IMMUNOTECHNIQUES

IMMUNOTECHNIQUES

By

Dr. Shivi Bhasin

(M.Sc., M.Phil., Ph. D.)

School of Studies in Zoology and Biotechnology

Vikram University, Ujjain (M.P.)

India

&

Dr. Arvind N. Shukla

(M.Sc., Ph. D.)

School of Studies in Zoology and Biotechnology

Vikram University, Ujjain (M.P.)

India

Published by:

DISCOVERY PUBLISHING HOUSE
4383/4B, Ansari Road, Darya Ganj
New Delhi-110 002 (India)
Phone : +91-11-23279245; 23253475; 43596065
E-mail : discoverybooksindia@gmail.com
discoverypublishinghouse@gmail.com
namitwasan9@gmail.com
web : www.discoverypublishinggroup.com

***First Edition:* 2023**

ISBN: 978-81-959169-6-2

Immunotechniques

Printed at:
Infinity Imaging Systems
Delhi

प्रो. अखिलेश कुमार पाण्डेय
कुलपति
Prof. Akhilesh Kumar Pandey
Vice Chancellor

विक्रम विश्वविद्यालय
नैक द्वारा 'ए' ग्रेड प्रदत्त
उज्जैन (म.प्र.) 456010 भारत
दूरभाष : 0734-2514270 (कार्यालय)
: 0734-2511071 (निवास)
फैक्स : 0734-2514276
VIKRAM UNIVERSITY
Accredited 'A' Grade by NAAC
Ujjain - 456010 (M.P.) India
Phone : 0734-2514270 (Off.)
: 0734-2511071 (Res.)
Fax : 0734-2514276
E-mail : vcvikramujn@gmail.com
Website : www.vikramuniv.ac.in

FOREWORD

I am extremely overwhelmed to write foreword of the book titled "Immunotechniques authored by Dr. Shivi Bhasin and Dr. Arvind N. Shukla. In, today's life the basic understanding of Immunity and immunology has been of uttermost importance. In the earlier publications made by the authors the authors have explained the type of Immune response generated by the body and various types of immune response generated against different viral attacks, the basic concept of immunology along with the general mechanism of immune response generation in a very simple and easy language. Immunology has always been an integral and inevitable part of modern Life-Sciences, the research carried out in this field and the terminology used in the subject is very challenging and intense, this however makes the subject a little tougher and difficult to understand. The book is a genuine attempt made by the authors to explain the different immune techniques like immunodiffuslon, immuno-electrophoresis, immunofluorescence, agglutination, RIA, ELISA, Mab etc. To make the book easy to understand, the book starts by explaining basic techniques like immuno-diffusion, immunoelectrophoresis and immuno-fluorescence etc. It must have been an uphill task for the authors to sum up such difficult terminology, into a simplified version. Authors have brought their years of experience in teaching and research to design this masterpiece in an easily understandable language. The material of the book is a knowledgeable and comprehensive collection of matter which will be helpful to all the students who wish to discover opportunities in this relatively new field of Life-Sciences. Readers of the book will definitely get deep insights about the wonderful field of immunology, including evident information regarding diagnostic techniques used of detection of Corona Virus. The book will be extremely beneficial to students, teachers and researchers working deeply in the field of Immunology, Zoology, Microbiology, Biochemistry, Medical Science and Biotechnology respectively.

I congratulate the authors for writing such useful and wonderful publication, and also wish them "All the Best" for their future endeavors.

15/12/22

(Akhilesh Kumar Pandey)

Preface

Immunology has emerged as one of the most exciting and demanding branch of science in 21st century. The current sanario, requires better and clear understanding of immunity and immune response generated by the body. Specially, in these COVID times, a detailed understanding of body's nature immune response is need of the hour. The study of immunology provides deep insight into the study of different components of immune system and their role in generation of immune response against the different types of viral infections. Immunology not only explains the different types of defense mechanism generated by the body but also explains the use of different immunomodulatory substances to enhance the capabilities of immune system. However, the basic of immunology also forms basis for the diagnosis of many diseases and also aids in the detection and treatment of many diseases. Deep understanding of the subject also allows to understand novel and innovative approaches in other important areas such as drug designing and development etc. To, realize the actual strength of immunology assistance from different scientific disciplines in a purposeful manner is required. Due to its interdisciplinary approach it attracts people from different diverse fields but the subject is a little tough with complicated terminologies.

The book is a genuine attempt to explain the basic concept of immunology, trying to simplify the language and the terminology of the subject. The book starts from explaining the different techniques of immunology like Immunodiffusion,

Immunoelectrophoresis, immunofluorescence, agglutination, RIA, ELISA, Mab etc. and is useful for students in UG and PG levels, we surprisingly noticed that there are very few books written by Indian authors which are competent enough to explain the complicated terminology, language of the subject and basic techniques of immunology, the book also assimilates the information in an understandable language. This prompted us to undertake this exciting and challenging project of writing a book "Immunotechniques" keeping in few the requirements of UG and PG courses of various Indian Universities. We claim no originality as we have extensively used various sources of information especially internet to compile and assimilate the vast socean of concepts and knowledge in order to give readers, the best. We also commit to bring somemore parts of the books to completely cover the entire stretch of the subject. We would like to thanks Prof. Akhilesh Kumar Pandey, Vice-chancellor, Vikram University, Ujjain, India for inspiring us to make such a composition. We are also extremely thankful to Dr. Salil Singh Head S.S. in Zoology and Biotechnology, Vikram University, Ujjain for providing necessary facilities for the completion of the book. We are also thankfully to our parents (Late Dr. Sudheer Bhasin, Mrs. Vijay Bhasin), relatives, friends and all other people directly or indirectly involved in bringing out this book.

Dr. Shivi Bhasin
Dr. Arvind N. Shukla

Contents

Immunodiffusion

INTRODUCTION

Immunodiffusion refers to an analytic technique in which reactants diffuse to intermingle with each other and react immunologically. More, specifically immunodiffusion refers to the movement of the antigen (Ag) and antibody molecules in a diffusion support medium. The technique is widely used for characterization and quantitation of antigens and antibodies (Ab) as it is easy to perform, give extremely valuable information and does not require elaborate equipment or reagents. The antibody has the ability to form precipitin lines with the Ag this forms the basis of the technique. The Ag and Ab diffuse in a gel which results in the formation of precipitate visible to naked eye.

Principle of Immunodiffusion

The initial concentration, shape and size of the molecule are decisive in determining the diffusion rate of any substance. If pore size in an inert gas is large, then condition for free diffusion can be closely approximated. In, general 1-2% agar from translucent gels is known universally to provide such conditions. The formation of visible precipitates between antigen and antibody is dependent inter alia, upon the concentration of the two reactants. In presence of excess of either, the immune complexes are usually soluble and the system thus requires optimum amount of both and has to be 'balanced'.

If the test tube is first lined up with Ab containing gel and then with another gel containing Ag, following which the entire set up is incubated for several hours. This leads to the formation of immune complexes, where both reactants diffuse into the intermediate gel, the size of these complexes then increases gradually and diffuse further to form a visible precipitate which is seen in the form of a "circular disc". On, the other hand when the size of the aggregate increases the pore size, no further migration takes place forming a "stationary band". The position of the band is dependent upon the initial concentrations of the antigen and antibody (Fig. 1.1).

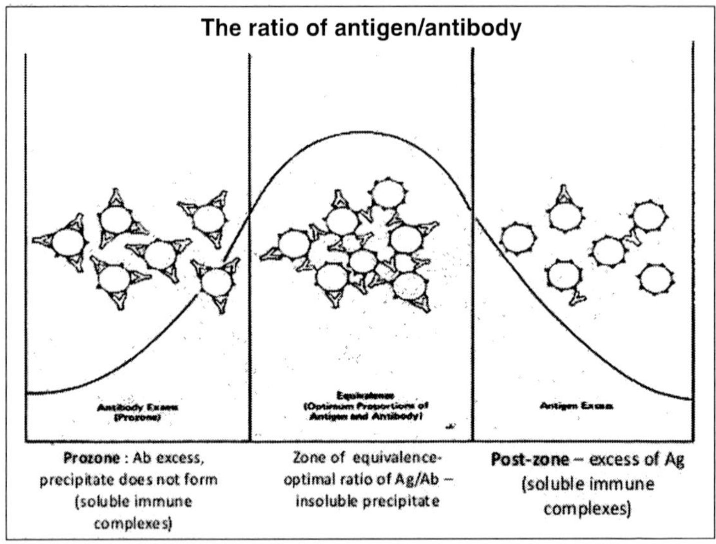

Fig. 1.1: Ratio of Antigen and Antibody

Procedure of Immunodiffusion

The procedure of immunodiffusion is performed in the following manner:

Plates: Generally, glass plates of rectangular in shape are used, size can vary according to nature of the experiment. Microscope slides (25×75mm) can be used for most routine work and for more specialized applications a glass plate of 70×100 or 100×100 mm can be used. These plates are uniform and without optical defects, should be designed in such a manner so that overheating can be avoided and should be cleaned and sterilized with ethanol.

Medium Used for Immunodiffusion: Agar or agarose is used to prepare gels, because of the neutrality of the gel, endosmosis is avoided and better results are seen in electrophoresis. However, commercially available crude agar may be purified by dissolving it at a concentration of 6% in boiling water and allowing it to solidify in a tall beaker. The bottom layer is removed and the rest is cut into small cubes which are then washed in running tap water for 3 days and then in distilled water for another 3 days. The solution can be dispensed in aliquots and kept at 4°C for several months, which is melted and diluted to 0.3 to 1% concentration with the appropriate buffer.

Buffers: For, techniques like immunodiffusion sodium phosphate buffer with pH around 7.1 and containing 0.15M sodium chloride (PBS) are used. The buffer is prepared by dissolving 2.76 g of diethyl barbituric acid in hot distilled water, 15.45 gm of sodium diethyl barbiturate is added and the solution is made up to 1L. The pH should be maintained around 8.6 as at this pH most proteins migrate towards the anode. Sodium azide at a final concentration of 0.1% should be added to the solution in order to prevent bacterial contamination during long periods of incubation.

Gel Solution: 1% agar or agarose is dissolved in PBS or barbital buffer by boiling with constant stirring. If necessary, the hot solution may be centrifuged to remove any particulate impurities.

The solution is cooled to 45-50° C in a water bath where the antibody has to be incorporated in the gels.

Gel Preparation: The plates are pre coated by dipping in 0.3% agar solution, followed by drying in open air. For, obtaining uniform gel plates the plates are considerably placed on a horizontal surface where gel solution is poured with a pre warmed glass pipette. A uniform gel is formed after sometime where, the thickness of the gel is around 1.5 mm. The plates after getting set are kept for few hours at 4° C in closed plastic box in humid conditions and with a layer of wet sponge.

Punching of Gel: The templates and punches used to make wells and troughs are commercially available or can be readily made. The template is made of 5-10mm thick "Prespex" sheet, containing holes of 2-4 mm which are drilled in various arrangements. The inter hole distance can vary between 4-10 mm where slits (50×2mm) are also made in template and wells are cut with punches made of steel tubes just fitting the holes. The gel-coated plates are kept aligned beneath the template and various arrangements of holes and troughs can be punched into the gel. The punched gel can be removed with a sharp needle or aspirated by connecting the well puncher to a water pump.

Sample Loading: The samples are prepared in the same buffer as that used in the gel, generally volumes of 3 to 10 μl can be loaded in 2-4 mm diameter wells and about 100 μl in the troughs. The wells or troughs should be completely filled with the sample to allow the formed precipitates to cover the entire thickness of the gel and to avoid artifacts of parallax. For quantitative applications, the volumes should be measured accurately with either a micro syringe or a constriction micropipette and wells should be loaded only once.

Incubation: Diffusion is allowed to proceed in a moist chamber where, humidity is maintained to prevent drying out of the gel during long incubations. The rate of diffusion is generally temperature dependent and for rapid development of precipitates the gels are incubated at room temperature overnight or at elevated temperatures up to

50° C for several hours. However, certain proteins liable in nature require incubation in cold for several days. In, case of large molecules like IgM development of precipitates is delayed due to long incubation. Continuous monitoring of plates is required to notice the development of immuno precipitate as, over incubation may sometimes lead to loss in sharpness of bands.

Staining: Staining of the precipitin bands is another important step in the process, after the development of the precipitin bands, the plates can be stained for improvement of sensitivity. Generally, the weak bands disappear in the process after which the plates are submerge in 0.15 m sodium chloride which, is changed regularly to remove non-precipitated proteins. The plates are kept in distilled water to remove excess of salt, after which gels are dried at 37 °C by keeping a wet filter paper over them. The gel is filled by a drop of agar solution to avoid cracking of jel and there after a suitable stain is used to stain the gel, the stain used for gel staining may include following:

(a) **Protein Stains:** These may include:

1. **Amido Black:** This contains 1% Amido Black in 7% acetic acid, the first staining should be done for 15-30 minutes, followed by a distain with 5% acetic acid the proteins here are stained dark blue.
2. **Coomassie Brilliant Blue R-250:** Coomassie Brilliant Blue is used by dissolving in ethanol, acetic acid and water (45:10:45 V/V) and then staining is done for 15-30 minutes. Then, the gel is de stained with ethanol, acetic acid, water (25:10:65V/V). This stain is about three times more sensitive than amido black and the proteins are stained blue by this stain.

(b) **Lipid Stains:** These may include:

Sudan Black: The Sudan black saturated solution is prepared in 60% ethanol at 37° C. The solution is filtered and 0.1 ml of 25% sodium hydroxide is added per 50ml dye just prior to use, the gel is stained for 2 hours and is de stained with 60% ethanol.

(c) **Carbohydrate Stains:** These may include following:

1. **Periodic acid Schiff's Stain:** This includes 1.5 g of basic fuchsin which is dissolved in 500 ml of boiling water. The gel is firstly stained with the above stain after which it is cooled to 55° C, then filtered and cooled further to 40° C. After this in the next step, 25ml of 2 N HCL and 3.75 h sodium meta bisulfide are respectively added to the mixture. Then, the salt dissolves and the gel is cooled and is stored at 4° C for 6 hours. The next step is addition of 1.2 g charcoal which is shaked for one minute to decolorize, then filtered rapidly and is stored at 4° C.

Record: The developed patterns can be recorded either by tracing using enlarger or by taking photographs in scattered light arrangement. The specific techniques are described below with brief procedures and special comments pertinent for execution and interpretation of results.

TYPES OF IMMUNODIFFUSION

When Ag and Ab diffuse towards each other in agar or when Ab is incorporated into agar and Ag diffuses into the Ab containing matrix, a clear and visible line of matrix is formed, the formation of this line takes place in the region of equivalence. Two frequently used immunodiffusion techniques are Radial immunodiffusion and Double immunodiffusion which, are carried out in a semi-solid agar medium.

(a) Radial Immunodiffusion (Mancini Method): In this technique, it is possible to make accurate quantitative determinations of the antigen even in very complex mixtures, e.g. individual classes of immunoglobulins in serum. The Ag is placed in a well and allowed to diffuse into agar containing a suitable dilution of an antiserum.

As, the Ag diffuses into agar, it reaches to the region of equivalence which is established and a ring of precipitation is formed around the well. The area of this ring is directly proportional to the concentration of Ag and the area of this ring is compared to standard curve, this leads to the determination of concentration of Ag sample (Fig. 1.2).

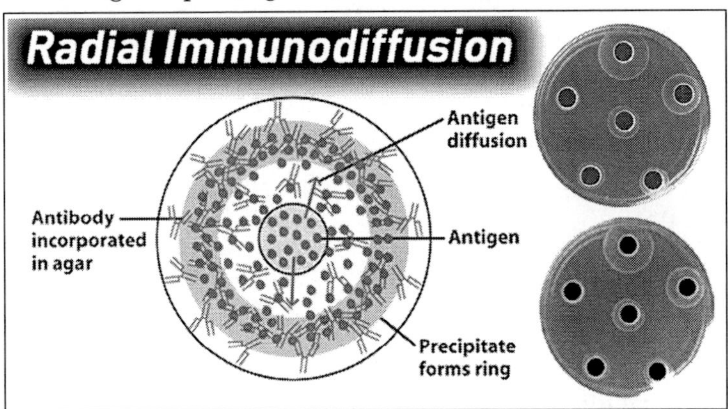

Fig. 1.2: Radial Immunodiffusion

Procedure: The procedure of single immunodiffusion can be summed up as:

1. A 2% melted agar solution (45-50° C) in PBS is mixed with an equal volume of pre warmed antiserum suitably diluted in the same buffer.
2. The mixture is poured over rectangular glass plates to give 1.5mm thick gel layer.
3. For accuracy and reproducibility of the method, it is important that the gel should be uniform.
4. Generally, wells of 2mm diameter are punched out with enough spacing to allow for unhindered development of precipitates.
5. Accurately, measured antigen reference solutions and samples are loaded into the wells and the plates are covered and incubated in a humid atmosphere until the precipitates become stationary.

6. The diameter of the circles can be measured either directly or after photography and the enlarged plates are also stained.
7. Final concentration of the antiserum to be used in the gel must be standardized for each batch of serum.
8. Generally, a final concentration of 1-5% high titre antiserum should be sufficed.
9. Decrease in the antiserum concentration leads to greater sensitivity and also leads to a decrease in the range of concentration.
10. Using this technique after staining it has been possible to estimate µg quantities of IgD in serum.
11. With further modifications using radio labelled antibody to the first antibody in the gel it has been possible to estimate 20-40ng of IgE in serum.

Applications of Radial Immunodiffusion: The technique of Radial immunodiffusion is used in:

1. Quantification of serum levels of IgM, IgG and IgA by incorporating class specific anti-isotype antibody into gel.
2. Determination of concentration of complement components in serum.
3. Determination of Ag sample by comparing the area of the precipitin ring with standard curve.

However, the biggest limitation of this technique is that it cannot detect antigens present in concentration below 5-10 µg/ml.

(b) Double Immunodiffusion: In this method both Ag and Ab diffuse towards each other, thus establishing a concentration gradient. On, reaching the equivalence a visible line of precipitation forms (Fig. 1.3).

Procedure: In case where two, different Ag preparations are placed in separate wells a different pattern of precipitin lines is observed which indicates that whether the two Ag share identical epitopes or not. The two precipitin lines which are formed are classified as:

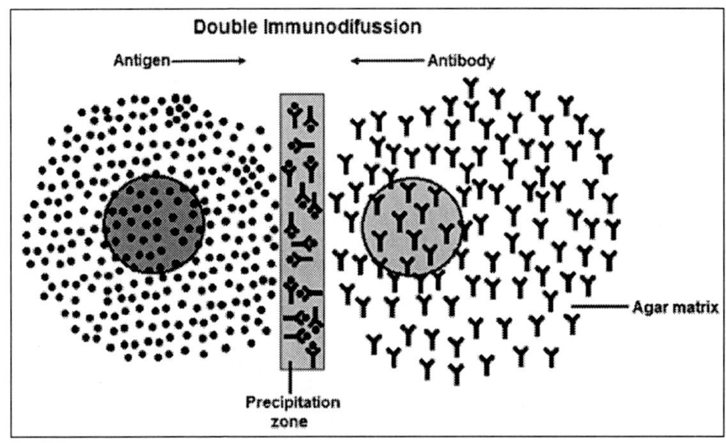

Fig. 1.3: Double Immunodiffusion

1. **Identity:** When two Ag share identical epitopes, the antiserum will form a single precipitin line, that will grow towards each other and will fuse to form a pattern called "Identity" (Fig. 1.4).

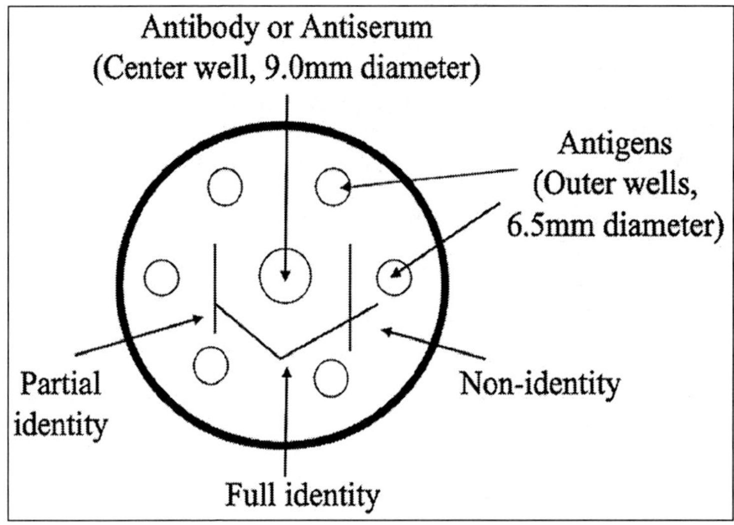

Fig. 1.4: Line of Identity

2. **Non-Identity:** When the two antigen are unrelated, the antiserum will form independent precipitin lines that cross each other and form a pattern called "non-identity". The lines are formed because the Ag and Ab do not precipitate and are hence free to diffuse (Fig. 1.5).

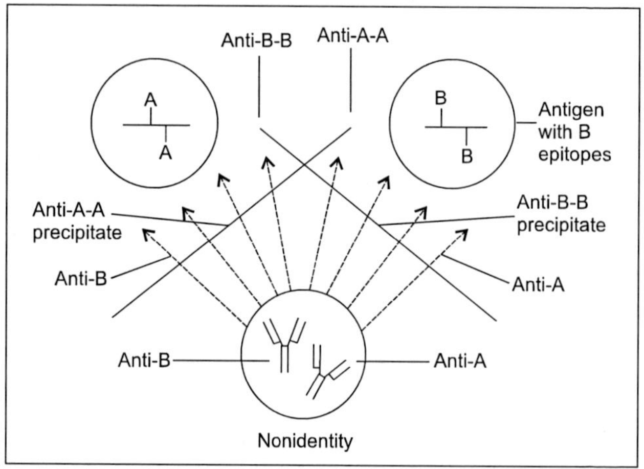

Fig. 1.5: Line of non-identity

3. **Partial Identity:** If two Ag share some epitope but one or the other has a unique epitope, the antibodies to common epitope form line of identity but Ab to the unique epitope diffuse the precipitin line to form a spur or a unique pattern known as "Partial Identity" (Fig. 1.6).

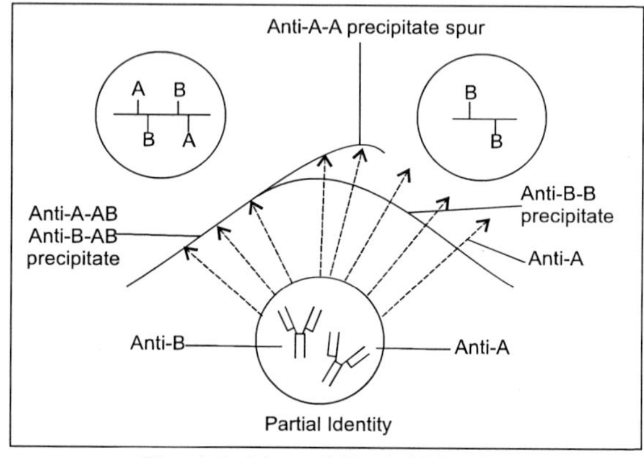

Fig. 1.6: Line of Partial Identity

APPLICATIONS

The technique has following applications:

1. The technique is used to study relationship between Ag and Ab.
2. The technique is used for quantitative estimation of Ag and Ab relationship.
3. It is used to determine the relative concentration of Ag or Ab.
4. It is also used to compare the relative epitopes of two antigens.
5. It is used to determine the relative purity of an Ag preparation.
6. It is also used for the diagnosis of various diseases.
7. It is also used for different serological surveys.

However, one of the major drawback of this method is that it takes 18-24 hour for the precipitin lines to appear.

POINTS TO REMEMBER

1. Immunodiffusion refers to an analytic technique in which reactants diffuse to intermingle with each other and react immunologically.
2. More, specifically immunodiffusion refers to the movement of the antigen (Ag) and antibody molecules in a diffusion support medium.
3. The initial concentration, shape and size of the molecule are decisive in determining the diffusion rate of any substance.
4. If pore size in an inert gas is large, then condition for free diffusion can be closely approximated.
5. When Ag and Ab diffuse towards each other in agar or when Ab is incorporated into agar and Ag diffuses into the Ab containing matrix, a clear and visible line of matrix is formed and the formation of this line takes place in the region of equivalence.

6. Two frequently used immunodiffusion techniques are Radial immunodiffusion and Double immunodiffusion which, are carried out in a semi-solid agar medium.

QUESTIONS

1. Explain in detail about immunodiffusion?
2. Explain the different types of immunodiffusion?
3. Explain in brief about radial immunodiffusion?
4. Explain in brief about double immunodiffusion?
5. Explain about the applications of immunodiffusion?

Immunoelectrophorosis

INTRODUCTION

Immunoelectrophorosis refers to precipitation in agar under electric field, it is a process which combines immunodiffusion and electrophoresis. The following techniques employ identification of the components of a complex antigen mixture, separated on the basis of charge, using formation of precipitin bands with specific antibody. Free diffusion leading to visible immune precipitates can be carried out after electrophoretic separation or in situ during the run. Considerable improvements in both resolution and sensitivity are possible over SRID and DID techniques employing only diffusion described earlier.

Agar or preferably agarose allow the gel to stabilize immediate diffusion of the separated components. Also if the gel retains its essential characteristics during electrophoresis, free diffusion leading to formation of precipitin bands can take place. Higher voltages give better and more rapid separation however, this also increases the resistance, generating more heat in the gels. As a result, the gel may get dehydrated and distortions are introduced in the final pattern. Heating may be reduced by limiting the ionic strength of the buffer and by cooling the plates from below, by circulation of water. If is also necessary to preserve humidity by carrying out the run in a covered apparatus.

PRINCIPLE

The rate of free diffusion of a substance in a solvent is mainly dependent upon the initial concentration, shape, size of the molecules and temperature of the entire set-up. If size of the pores in an inert gel and is sufficiently large, the conditions for free diffusion can be closely approximated, 1-2% agar or agarose from translucent gels are universally used for the process.

The formation of visible precipitates between antigen is dependent inter alia, upon the concentration of the two reactants. In presence of excess of either, the immune complexes are usually soluble, the system thus has to be 'balanced'.

Buffers of molarity up to 0.1 and a pH range of 7-8 are employed. If a gel incorporating antibody (in a test tube) is first layered with plain gel solution, then with another gel containing the antigen and the whole is incubated for several hours, immune complexes are formed as both the reactants diffuse into intermediate gel. These complexes rapidly increase in size with further diffusion and aggregate to form a visible precipitate seen as a circular disc. When the aggregates become larger than the pores of the gel, no further migration takes place and a stationary band is obtained. The position of the band is dependent upon the initial concentrations of the antigen and antibody. For greater sensitivity and ease of manipulation the procedure is carried out on a plate layered with the agar gel where wells or troughs are cut into the gel for loading solutions.

GENERAL PROCEDURES

Uniform gel layers are prepared on glass plates as described earlier using barbital buffer, wells and troughs are punched using the template in the desired arrangement.

The run is carried out in an apparatus shown schematically and same barbital buffer is used for gels which is then poured to an equal level in both electrode chambers. Connections between gel and electrodes are made through whatman filter paper wicks wetted with buffer and the wicks are placed about 3mm on the ends of the gels. The lid is closed and run and are carried out up to 6 hours with 5-10 V/cm or overnight at 2V/cm gel. Bromophenol blue dye binds to serum albumin and can be used as an internal marker to monitor the run.

Components migrating towards the cathode (eg. lgG) or migrating slowly towards the anode can be carbamylated to improve anodic migration. The reaction is carried out at 45° C for 30 min with an equal volume of 2M potassium cyanate. The sample is cooled to 10-15° C in water bath and diluted to desired concentration with barbaital buffer (Fig. 2.1).

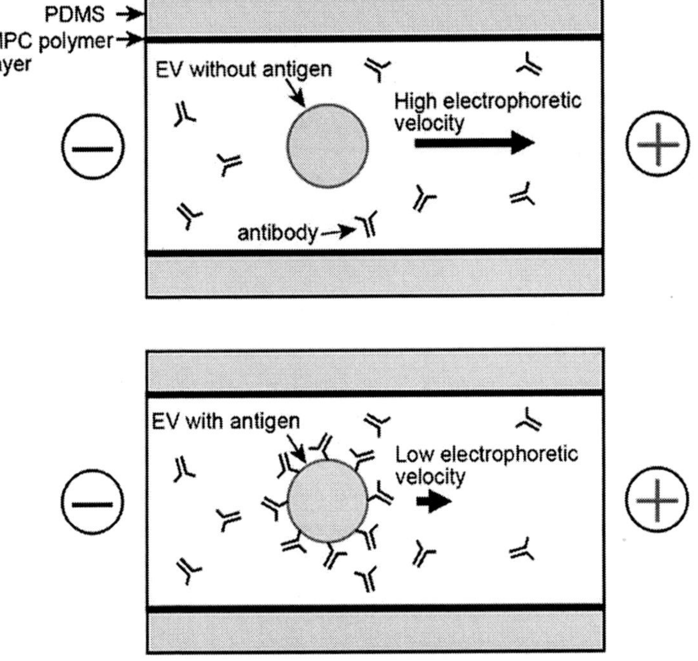

Fig. 2.1: Process of Immunoelectrophorosis

Plates: Generally, glass plates of rectangular shape are used, size can vary according to nature of the experiment. Microscope slides (25×75mm) can be used for most routine work and for more specialized application a glass plate of 70×100 or 100×100 mm can be used. These plates are uniform, without optical defects and should be designed in such a manner so that overheating can be avoided, also cleaning and sterilization of the plates with ethanol should be maintained on regular basis.

Medium used for immunoelectrophorosis: Agar or agarose is used to prepare gels, because the neutrality of the gel, avoids electro endosmosis and shows better results in electrophoresis. However, commercially available crude agar may be purified by dissolving it at a concentration of 6% in boiling water and allowing it to solidify in a tall beaker. The bottom layer is removed and the rest cut into small cubes and are washed in a running tap water for 3 days and are then run in distilled water for another 3 days. The solution can be dispensed in aliquots and is kept at 4° C for several months, which is melted and diluted to 0.3 at 1% concentration with the appropriate buffer.

Buffers: For, techniques like immunodiffusion sodium phosphate buffer with pH around 7.1 and containing 0.15M sodium chloride (PBS) is used. The buffer is prepared by dissolving 2.76 g of diethyl barbituric acid in hot distilled water, 15.45 g of sodium diethyl barbiturate is added and the solution is made up to 1L. The pH should be 8.6 and at this pH most proteins migrate towards the anode. Sodium azide at a final concentration of 0.1% should be added to prevent bacterial contamination during long periods of incubation.

Gel Solution: 1% agar or agarose is dissolved in PBS or barbital buffer by boiling with constant stirring. If, necessary the hot solution may be centrifuged to remove any particulate impurities. The solution is then cooled to 45-50° C in a water bath where the antibody is incorporated in the gels.

Gel Preparation: The plates are pre coated by dipping in 0.3% agar solution, followed by drying in open air. For, obtaining uniform gel plates the plates are considerably placed on a horizontal surface where gel solution is poured with a pre warmed glass pipette. A uniform gel is formed after sometime where, the thickness of the gel is around 1.5 mm. The plates after getting set are kept for few hours at 4° C in closed plastic box in humid conditions and with a layer of wet sponge.

Punching of gel: The templates and punches used to make wells and troughs are commercially available or can be readily made. The template is made of 5-10mm thick "Prespex" sheet, containing holes of 2-4 mm which are drilled in various arrangements. The inter hole distance can vary between 4-10 mm where slits (50×2mm) are also made in template and wells are cut with punches made of steel tubes just fitting the holes. The gel-coated plates are kept aligned beneath the template and various arrangements of holes and troughs can be punched into the gel. The punched gel can be removed with a sharp needle or aspirated by connecting the well puncher to a water pump.

Sample Loading: The samples are prepared in the same buffer as that used in the gel, generally volumes of 3 to 10 µl can be loaded in 2-4 mm diameter wells and about 100 µl in the troughs. The wells or troughs should be completely filled with the sample to allow the formed precipitates to cover the entire thickness of the gel and to avoid artifacts of parallax. For quantitative applications, the volumes should be measured accurately with either a micro syringe or a constriction micropipette and wells should be loaded only once.

Incubation: Diffusion is allowed to proceed in a moist chamber where, humidity is maintained to prevent drying out of the gel during long incubations. The rate of diffusion is generally temperature dependent and for rapid development of precipitates the gels are incubated at room temperature overnight or at elevated temperatures up to

50° C for several hours. However, certain proteins liable in nature require incubation in cold for several days. In, case of large molecules like IgM development of precipitates is delayed due to long incubation. Continuous monitoring of plates is required to notice the development of immuno precipitate as, over incubation may sometimes lead to loss in sharpness of bands.

Staining: Staining of the precipitin bands is another important step in the process, after the development of the precipitin bands, the plates can be stained for improvement of sensitivity. Generally, the weak bands disappear in the process after which the plates are submerge in 0.15 m sodium chloride which, is changed regularly to remove non-precipitated proteins. The plates are kept in distilled water to remove excess of salt, after which gels are dried at 37° C by keeping a wet filter paper over them. The gel is filled by a drop of agar solution to avoid cracking of jel and there after a suitable stain is used to stain the gel, the stain used for gel staining may include following:

(a) **Protein Stains:** These may include:

1. **Amido Black:** This contains 1% amido Black in 7% acetic acid, the first staining should be done for 15-30 minutes, followed by a distain with 5% acetic acid, the proteins here are stained dark blue.
2. **Coomassie Brilliant Blue R-250:** Coomassie Brilliant Blue is used by dissolving in ethanol, acetic acid and water (45:10:45 V/V) and then staining is done for 15-30 minutes. Then, the gel is de stained with ethanol, acetic acid, water (25:10:65V/V). This stain is about three times more sensitive than amido black and the proteins are stained blue by this stain.

(b) **Lipid Stains:** These may include:

Sudan Black: The Sudan black saturated solution is prepared in 60% ethanol at 37° C. The solution is filtered and 0.1 ml of 25% sodium hydroxide is added per 50ml dye just prior to use, the gel is stained for 2 hours and is de stained with 60% ethanol.

(c) **Carbohydrate Stains:** These may include following:

1. **Periodic acid Schiff's Stain:** This includes 1.5 g of basic fuchsin which is dissolved in 500 ml of boiling water. The gel is firstly stained with the above stain after which it is cooled to 55° C, then filtered and cooled further to 40° C. After this bin the next step, 25ml of 2 N HCL and 3.75 h sodium meta bisulphite is added. Then, the salt dissolves after which the gel is cooled and is stored at 4° C for 6 hours. The next step is the addition of 1.2 g charcoal which is shaked for one minute to decolorize, then filtered rapidly and is stored at 4° C.

Record: The developed patterns can be recorded either by tracing using enlarger or by taking photographs in scattered light arrangement. The specific techniques are described below with brief procedures and special comments pertinent to execution and interpretation of results.

Types of Immunoelctrophorosis: The immune electrophoretic techniques employ identification of components of a complex, using formation of precipitin bands with specific antibody. Free diffusion leading to visible immune precipitates can be carried out after electrophoretic separation or in situ during the run. Agar or agarose allow gel to stabilize immediate diffusion of separate components. Some of the main electrophoresis are following:

ROCKET IMMUNOELECTROPHORESIS (RIE)

This technique is basically similar to single Radial Immunodiffusion (SRID) except that a considerable increase in sensitivity and time is obtained by making the antigen migrate in an electric field into an antibody containing gel. The antigen combines immediately with the antibody to form immune complexes and the complexes continue migration, albeit at a slower rate. Migration stops completely when the aggregates become larger enough to be retained by the pores of the gel. The area under the precipitate, which take the shape of a 'rocket' can be closely approximated to a triangle. As all wells are of an equal diameter (base of the 'rocket') the height of the peaks is proportional to the area. The height shows a linear proportionality with the concentration of the antigen. By running reference solutions and unknown samples on the same plate, the concentration of the unknown samples can be determined.

Procedure

Uniform gel layers incorporating a monospecific antiserum are made as described for SRID, except for use of barbital buffer in this case. Wells of equal diameter are punched at an inter well distance of about 0.8 cm and the samples are rapidly loaded in duplicate with the current on at 2V/cm. The current here after is increased to 8-10V/cm and is passed for 4-6 hours here the peak heights should be between 10-50 mm for accurate measurements.

The final concentration of antiserum in the gel and reference antigen concentration have to be standardized for each system. As with SRID, an increase in sensitivity, with a concomitant narrowing the estimable range is achieved by lowering the antiserum concentration. Poly specific antisera show multiple peaks, simultaneous estimation of two or more components can be made if the peaks can be identified using suitable reference antigens. For substances migrating in both directions (e.g. IgG) or showing very little migration it is better to carry out estimations after carbamylation of both reference and unknown solutions (see Procedure for immune electrophoretic technique). Using a poly specific serum and closely spaced wells, the technique has been used to analyse fractions from column effluents. The patterns are called 'fused rockets and a serological analysis can be made of eluted antigens with sensitivity less than 1μg/ml of the antigen that has been obtained after staining the plates (Fig. 2.2).

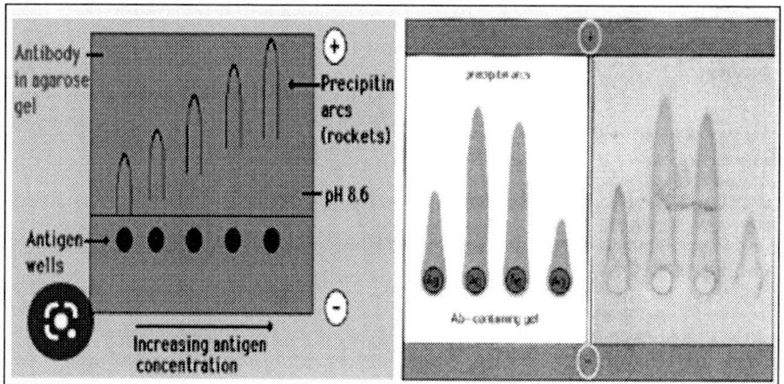

Fig. 2.2: Rocket Immunoelectrophorosis

IMMUNOELECTROPHORESIS (IE)

This technique is actually a combination of ordinary electrophoresis of a complex mixture of antigens and subsequent identification of the separated components by double immunodiffusion with the antiserum in the same gel. Unlike double immunodiffusion in wells, the separated fractions are not well defined and the precipitin bands take the shape of arcs. The same basic reactions between two antigens can develop here also where the arrangement of the samples in wells and troughs can be adjusted to facilitate comparisons between reference and unknown samples. With electrophoresed normal human serum precipitin bands developed with an antiserum raised against whole serum, up to 15-20 bands which can be easily identified.

Procedure

Wells are punched out in gel plates prepared in barbital buffer as troughs spaced at 2-8 mm from the well parallel to the directions of run which can be punched at the same time. The gel is not removed from the troughs at this stage as it may introduce in consistencies in the current. After the run (5-10 V/cm), adjudged empirically or by migration of bromophenol blue dye the, troughs are emptied of the gel and filled to brim with the antiserum (50-100µl), the plates are then incubated to allow the development of immune precipitates.

This technique has been used extensively for identification of an abnormal increase or decrease in one component amongst many present in a complex mixture. Such clinical situations like myelomas or immune deficiencies where one or more of more of immunoglobulin classes can register an abnormal increase or decrease which has been recognized, like double immunodiffusion, the technique is at best only semi quantitatively (Fig. 2.3).

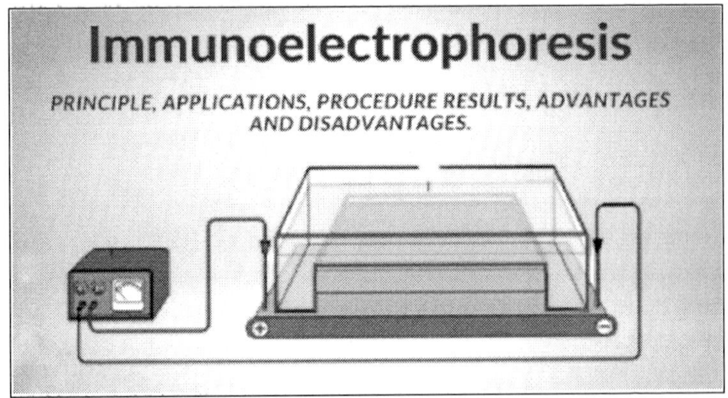

Fig. 2.3: Immunoelectrophorosis

CROSSED IMMUNOELECTROPHORESIS (CIE)

This is the most sophisticated of all techniques described here utilizing the principles of immuno-precipitation. It involves two stages, in the first stage the complex antigen mixture is electrophoresed as in IE. The separated components are then electrophoresed again in a second dimension, at right angles to the first, into another gel incorporating the antiserum as in RIE. The resultant precipitin patterns, can give serological information about the antigen mixture. As all the material is used information of immune precipitates, the area under each peak is proportional to the antigen concentration. The area can be determined either by counting squares after tracing or by polarimetry. Again, understanding of the basic reactions described for DID makes it possible to have numerous variants suited for further analysis of the system.

Procedure

Addition of Ca^{2+} to barbital buffer is recommended for better results, the buffer is prepared by dissolving 2.07g of diethyl barbituric acid in about 100 ml distilled water after which mixture is boiled and 13.14 gm of sodium diethyle barbiturate, 0.4 g of calcium lactate, 0.2 gm sodium azide are then added and the volume is made up to 1 liter. Before use, the buffer is diluted 1:5 with distilled water and wells are punched, samples are loaded and run is carried out as for immune electrophoresis. To avoid cathodic migration, the samples can be carbamylated, after the run, the edges of the gel are sliced with a sharp rectangular blade. The gel is lifted with the help of the blade and placed on to the edge of another plate. Antiserum containing gel solution (RIE) is then poured to cover rest the plate. If intermediate gels have to be used, a barrier such as a brass block can be used to limit the area of application. After congealing of the gel, the barrier is removed after cutting off the adhering gel. The next gel solution is then poured and the second run is carried out overnight at angles to the first at 2V/cm, the plates are usually stained after the second run as described earlier.

Using this technique, it has been possible to identify and characterize complex antigenic patterns with sera from patients infected with microbial organisms. Also, protein changes can be followed during disease. Hereditary polymorphism and micro heterogeneity etc. can be analyzed with this method (Fig. 2.4).

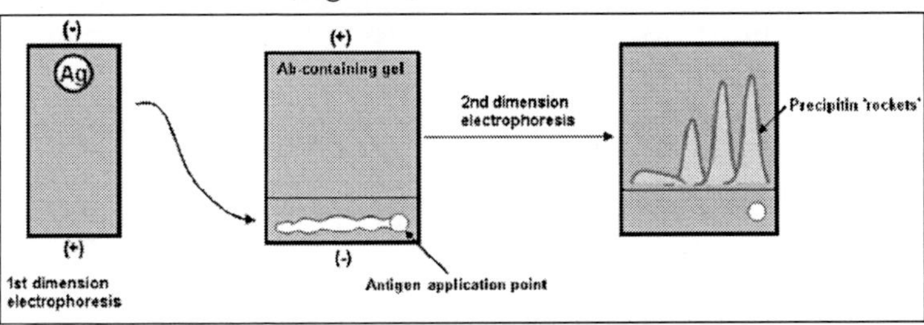

Fig. 2.4: Crossed Immuno electrophoresis

Applications of Immunoelectrophorosis:

1. This technique helps in the identification and approximate quantization of various proteins in serum.
2. It works in the identification of normal and abnormal proteins and is used in patients with suspected monoclonal and polyclonal gammopathies.
3. The technique is used to analyse complex protein mixtures containing different antigens.
4. The method is used to monitor Ag-Ab purity to identify a single Ag in a mixture of Ag.
5. The technique is also used for qualitative analysis of M-proteins in serum and urine.
6. Imuno electrophoresis aids in the diagnosis and evaluation of the therapeutic response in many disease states affecting the immune system.

POINTS TO REMEMBER

1. Immuno electrophoresis refers to precipitation in agar under electric field, it is a process which combines immune-diffusion and electrophoresis.
2. The following techniques employ identification of the components of a complex antigen mixture, separated on the basis of charge, using formation of precipitin bands with specific antibody.
3. The rate of free diffusion of a substance in a solvent is mainly dependent upon the initial concentration, shape and size of the molecules and the temperature.
4. The immune electrophoretic techniques employs identification of components of a complex, using formation of precipitin bands with specific antibody.
5. Free diffusion leading to visible immune precipitates can be carried out after electrophoretic separation or in situ during the run.

QUESTIONS

1. Explain in detail about electrophoretic technique?
2. Explain the main principle behind electrophoretic technique?
3. Explain about different types of electrophoresis?
4. Write a short note on rocket electrophoresis?
5. Write a short note on crossed electrophoresis?
6 Explain the different applications of electrophoresis?

Immunofluorescence

INTRODUCTION

Immunofluorescence may be define as an immunoassay which detects the presence of antigen (Ag) in biological specimen sample or vice-versa. It was first discovered in 1942 and was redefined by Coons in 1950, the technique involves use of a fluorescence microscope which is able to read the specific immunological reaction and cellular slide preparations. The specificity of antibodies to their antigen is the base for immunofluorescence and the technique is used as an effective method for visualizing intracellular processes, structures and conditions like in vitro type of Ag-Ab interaction, the technique is also applied in the detection of surface antigens or antibodies.

PRINCIPLE OF IMMUNOFLUORESCENCE

In this technique the specific antibodies are first bound to the antigen or protein of interest. The antibodies are generally labelled with molecules having the property of fluorescence which are known as fluorochromes. When light one wavelength falls on fluorochrome, it absorbs that light to emit light of another wavelength and the emitted light can be viewed with a fluorescence microscope. The property of certain dyes absorbing light rays at one particular wavelength (ultraviolet light) and emitting them at a different wavelength (visible light) is the base of the reaction. The dye usually used is fluorescein isothiocyanate, which gives yellow-green fluorescence (Fig. 3.1), this technique is also known as "**Fluorescent Antibody Tests**" (FAT).

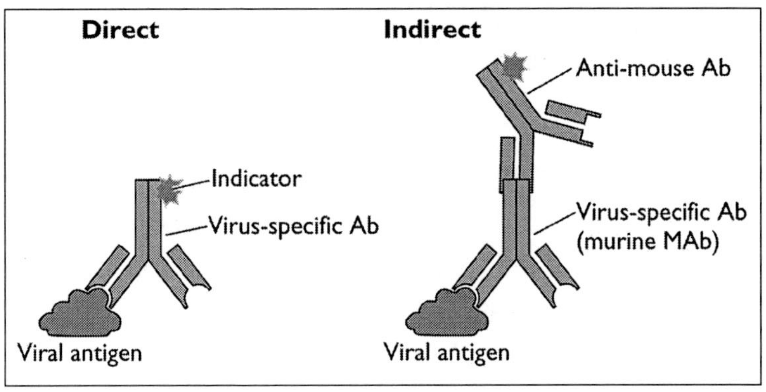

Fig. 3.1: Immunofluorescence Technique

Requirements of Immunofluorescence: There are certain requirements of Immunofluorescence which include following:

(a) **Primary Antibody:** The primary Ab is an Ab which binds directly with the Ag.

(b) **Secondary Antibody:** The Ab which binds to the Fc region of a primary Ab that is already bound with specific Ag and It is effectively used for different types of assays.

(c) **Fluorescent Dye:** A fluorescent dye or fluorchrome or fluorophore is a molecule which is conjugated to Ab, commonly used fluorchromes are fluorescein, rhodamine and phycoerythrin.

(d) **Immunofluorescence Microscope:** It is required for visualization.

(e) **Wash Buffers:** Wash buffers such as PBS (Phosphate Buffered Saline) are used which help to wash unbound antibodies.

Types of Immunofluorescence: There are basically two types of Immunofluorescence they include:

1. **Direct Immunofluorescence:** It is a type of test in which single Ab i.e. primary Ab is used which is generally chemically linked to a fluorochrome and if Ag is present the primary Ab reacts with it and fluorescence can be observed under the fluorescent microscope (Fig. 3.2).

Procedure of Direct Immunofluorescence: The steps of direct Immunofluorescence involve following:

1. The specimen is firstly fixed into the slide.
2. After, this fluorochrome labelled antibodies are then added to the slide.
3. Then, the slide is carefully washed with buffers like PBS in order to remove other components except for the complex of Ag and flurochrome- labelled Ab.
4. The slide is then observed under a fluorescent microscope.

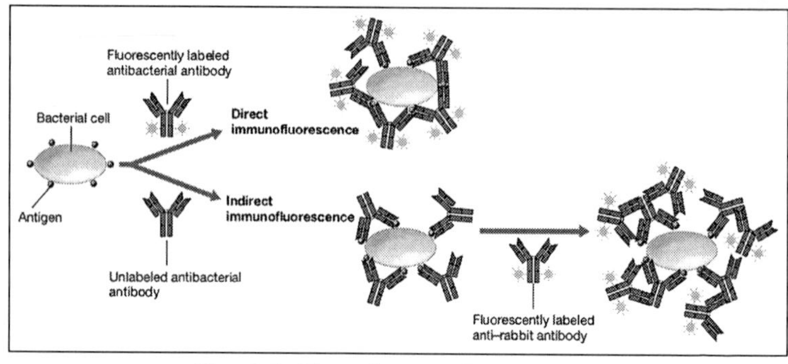

Fig. 3.2: Direct Immunofluorescence

Applications and Advantages of Direct Immunofluorescence: The technique implies numerous applications as:

1. It is used in the detection of rabies virus Ag in the skin smear collected from nape of the neck in humans and saliva of dogs.

2. It is successfully used in the detection of *N. gonorrhoeae C. diphtheria* and *T. pallidium* etc. directly in appropriate clinical specimens.
3. Protocols for direct IF are usually shorter as they require only one labelling step.
4. Species cross-reactivity is minimized indirect methods as the fluorophore is already conjugated to the primary Ab.

Disadvantages of Direct Immunofluorescence Test: There are some disadvantages of these techniques they include:

1. This method requires separately labelled antibodies which are prepared for each pathogen.
2. This method requires the use of primary Ab in high amount which is extremely expensive.
3. It is a less sensitive method than indirect Immunofluorescence.

Indirect Immunofluorescence: In this technique double antibodies i.e. primary and secondary antibodies are used. The primary Ab is not labeled however, a fluorochrome-labeled secondary Ab is used for detection. The Ag used is known and it binds to the specific primary Ab of interest in the sample. The secondary Ab then binds to the Fc region of primary Ab (Fig. 3.3).

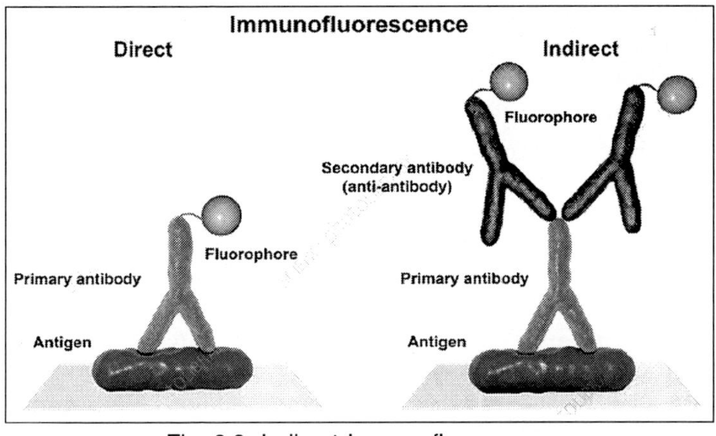

Fig. 3.3: Indirect Immunofluorescence

Procedure of Indirect Immunofluorescence: The procedure of Indirect Immunofluorescence is as follows:

1. Fixing of a known Ag on a slide.
2. The specimen to be tested is applied to the slide.
3. The slide is incubated and carefully wash with PBS.
4. A secondary Ab (eg. fluorescently labelled anti-IgG) is added.
5. The slide is washed and is again washed with PBS.
6. The slide is then observed under fluorescence microscope.

Applications and Advantages of Immunofluorescence: The technique has several applications and advantages which include following:

1. It is used for the detection of specific Ab for diagnosis of syphilis, amoebiasis, leptospirosis, toxoplasmosis and other diseases.
2. The technique is used in the detection of autoantibodies that cause auto immune diseases.
3. In this technique a single fluorochrome labelled antibody is used for detecting many Ag-Ab interaction.
4. It is a sensitive technique than direct immunofluorescence test.
5. In this, multiple secondary Ab can bind to the Fc region of primary Ab which amplifies the fluorescence signal.

Disadvantages of Indirect Immunofluorescence test: The technique implies many disadvantages:

1. It is more complex and time-consuming than the direct IF.
2. Cross-reactivity of secondary antibody to other agents can be problematic.

Interpretation of Immunofluorescence: If there is presence of a specific Ag or Ab, it will form Ag-Ab complex. So, the fluochrome-conjugate Ab will remain bound in preparation even after washing and fluorescence of yellow - green or red can be observed while visualizing through a fluorescent microscope and the test can be considered positive.

APPLICATIONS OF IMMUNOFLUORESCENCE

There are some major applications of Immunofluorescence these include:

1. Immunofluorescence can be used on tissues or cell sections to determine presence of different biological molecules.
2. It is also used in molecular biology for visualization of cytoskeleton such as intermediate filaments.
3. It also plays a key role in the detection of autoimmune disorders.
4. It can be used with some non-antibody methods of florescent staining like the use of DAPI (4, 6-diamidino-2-phenylindole) to label DNA.

Limitations of Immunofluorescence: There are some limitations of the technique which include:

1. The main problem in use of this technique is photoleaching i.e. degradation of flurochromes and can be prevented by using higher concentration of flurochromes and decreasing exposure time to light.
2. Extraneous unnecessary fluorescence can occur due to impurity of targeted antigens.
3. Auto fluorescence can occur due to some agents which bear the property of fluorescence in the given specimen.
4. It is mostly used for only fixed or dead cells.
5. It is expensive and require higher expertise.

Flow Cytometry: Flow Cytometry is a process where individual cells or other biological particles which are made to pass in a single file, in a fluid stream by a sensor or sensors which measure physical or chemical characteristics of cells or particles. However, modern flow cytometry is the result of applications is the result of applications of cytochemical staining, monoclonal antibody production, flourochrome chemistry, laser technology and computer aided data processing.

Equipment Required for Flow Cytometry: Flow cytometer FAC Scan (Becton Dickinson), low speed refrigerated centrifuge with swing or rotor. Simulant control (IgG_1-FITC+IgG2a-PE), simulant for T and B cells, simulant for CD_4/CD_8+ T cells, Ficoll-hypaque (Pharmacia), RPMI 1640, RPMI containing 10% FCS and 0.1% NaN, RPMI 1640 containing 0.1% NaN_3, Propidium iodine 1 mg/ml stock solution, Falcon tube 12×75 mm.

Procedure: The procedure of flow cytometry is as follows:

1. Draw 15-20 ml of blood from a volunteer by venepuncture into heparinized tubes. Separate the mononuclear cells (PBMC) over ficoll hypaque gradient following the usual procedure.
2. Resuspend cells in 10 ml of RPMI 1640, after counting in a haemocytometer, adjust the cell number to 1 million cells per ml. Distribute 1 ml of cell suspension in Felcon tubes (labelled properly).
3. Dilute the monoclonal antibodies in RPMI 1640 containing 10% FCS and 0.1% NAN_2.
4. Pellet down cells and aspirate the supernatant and all washing should be carried out at 4° C.
5. Disturb the cell pellet by gentle tapping and add 100 µl of diluted monoclonal antibodies as following:

   Tube 1- Simultest control

   Tube 2- Simultest for T and B cells

   Tube 3- Simultest for CD_4 and CD_8
6. Incubate at 4° C in ice for 30-45 minutes.
7. Wash cells with 1ml of chilled RPMI 1640 containing 0.1%NaN3 by centrifugation to remove unbound antibodies.
8. Resuspend, cells in 500 µl or RPMI 1640 and keep the tubes protected from light until analysis.
9. Determination the percent of dead cells, add propidium iodide in tube 1 to a final concentrate of 5 µg/ml, 5-10 minutes before analysing the sample in FAC Scan (Fig. 3.4).

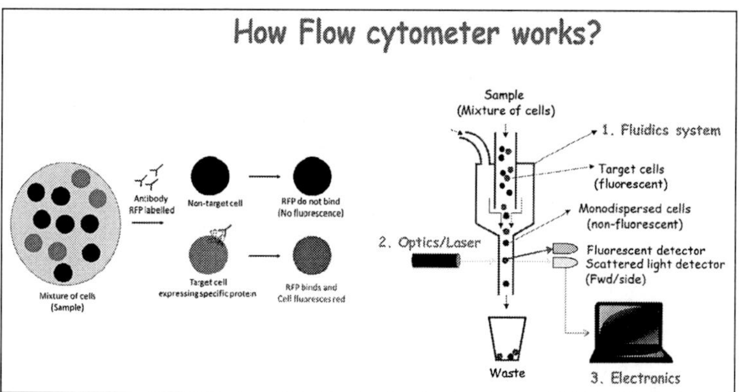

Fig. 3.4: Flow Cytometry

Sample Analysis: The samples are acquired in FAC Scan using Consort 30 or FACS Scan can research software and the basic principles described here are essentially similar for other flow cytometry system.

1. Acquire events using cells in tube 1 for setting up the instruments, adjust the forward scatter (FSC) and 90° side scatter detector (SSC) levels to position the lymphocytes, monocytes, containing RBC and debris on the plot display.
2. During, acquisition of data from cells in tube 1, adjust the FL 1 detector level to bring the unstained cell population to the left end of the histogram display and repeat the same for FL2 channel. As, the fluorescence intensity for cell surface molecules is generally 5-6 times more than that of background the samples are acquired using logarithmic amplification.
3. To, determine the percentage of dead cells in cell preparation, set up a dot plot display with FSC in the X axis and FL2 on the Y axis using tube 1. Dead cells will take up propidium iodide and fluoresce with high intensity at FL-2. Dead cells and debris can be excluded during acquisition by setting a live gate.

4. The instruments setting is carried in steps 1, 2 and 3, mutually exclusive T and B cell markers are used for setting fluorescence compensation. Set up FL1 & FL2 on the dot plot display and adjust FL2-% FL1 compensation such that FITC labelled cells which have the same mean Y values as the unlabelled population. Similarly, adjust FL1-%FL2 compensation such that PE labelled cells have the same mean X value as the unlabelled cells.
5. With the same instruments setting acquire 10,000 events from each of the 3 tubes and the data is saved for analysis.
6. Using, data from tube 1, a gate for lymphocyte population in FSC vs SSC is set and is displayed to exclude dead cells and debris.
7. The quadrant markers in FL1 vs FL2 display to delineate the negative population.
8. Dual parameter displayed for tube 2 and 3 to determine the proportion of T, B i.e. CD_4+ and CD_8+ cells respectively.

Precaution to be taken in Flow Cytometry: Following precautions should be taken in the process of flow cytometry:

1. The count of dead cells should be restricted as it should not exceed 10% of total cells, the sample should be rejected.
2. When, the contaminating cell population is more, data can be acquired by gating the required population.
3. The fluorescence seen in the control sample is due to autofluorescence, it is utmost importance to set the fluorescence detector levels using the labelled cell population.
4. The sample should be in a single suspension.
5. The labelled tube should have to be stored in paraformaldehyde and propidium iodide should not be used.

POINTS TO REMEMBER

1. Immunofluorescence may be define as an immunoassay which detects the presence of antigen (Ag) in biological specimen sample or vice-versa.
2. The specificity of antibodies to their antigen is the base for immunofluorescence and the technique may be used as an effective method for visualizing intracellular processes, structures and conditions like in vitro type of Ag-Ab interaction.
3. In this technique the specific antibodies are first bound to the antigen or protein of interest and the antibodies are generally labelled with molecules having the property of fluorescence which are known as fluorochromes.
4. When light one wavelength falls on fluorochrome, it absorbs that light to emit light of another wavelength and the emitted light can be viewed with a fluorescence microscope.
5. The property of certain dyes absorbing light rays at one particular wavelength (ultraviolet light) and emitting them at a different wavelength (visible light) is the base of the reaction.
6. The dye usually used is fluorescein isothiocyanate, which gives yellow-green fluorescence this technique is also known as "**Fluorescent Antibody Tests** (FAT).

QUESTIONS

1. Explain about immunofluorescence in detail?
2. Explain the method of immunofluorescence?
3. Explain the different types of immunofluorescence?
4. Explain about direct immunofluorescence?
5. Explain about indirect immunofluorescence?
6. Explain the different applications of immunofluorescence?

Agglutination

INTRODUCTION

Antigen-Antibody (Ag-Ab) interact in such a way that they generate visible clumping, this reaction or clumping is referred as agglutination. It is a highly sensitive reaction and the antibodies which produce agglutination are called "Agglutinins". These agglutinins are capable of reacting with bacterial cells, white blood cells or RBC's as agglutination results in formation of flocculent masses or compact granules which are visible by naked eyes. Agglutination occurs optimally when antibodies or agglutinins react with particulate antigen in equivalent proportion. Agglutination reaction is one method to put an evidence of antigen antibody interaction where there is a specific antibody to an antigen present on surface of particles. The reaction takes place as a result of particles coming together and producing a visible clumping (agglutination). The particles can be bacteria, cells of higher plants or animals, micro fungi, or Rickettsia. Synthetic polymer particles like latex, bentonite and collodion can also be agglutinated after attachment of antigens on their surface. The particle should have a size greater than 200-250 nm to produce a visible reaction.

Reaction time for agglutination reaction is short, from a few minutes to a few hours at the most, the reaction is sensitive enough for demonstration of as little as 10^{-} to $10^{-}\times$ gram of antibody.

MECHANISM OF AGGLUTINATION

Beyond this zone presence of excess of antigen or antibody inhibit the agglutination reaction, this inhibitory effect is known as "Prozone Effect". The agglutination reaction is brought about by the linking of Ag and Ab, generally antibodies are bivalent so, one Ab can link two adjacent Ag. The IgM Ab is multivalent and it contains 5 or 10 combining sites and hence it can link many antigens at one time, but different antibodies have different combining capacities for example, IgM antibody has capacity for lump formation with a lesser number of molecules than that of IgG antibody molecules. The antibodies which carry a single combining site is unable to form lump or lattice and hence agglutination will not occur (Fig. 4.1). The mechanism of agglutination can be summed up as:

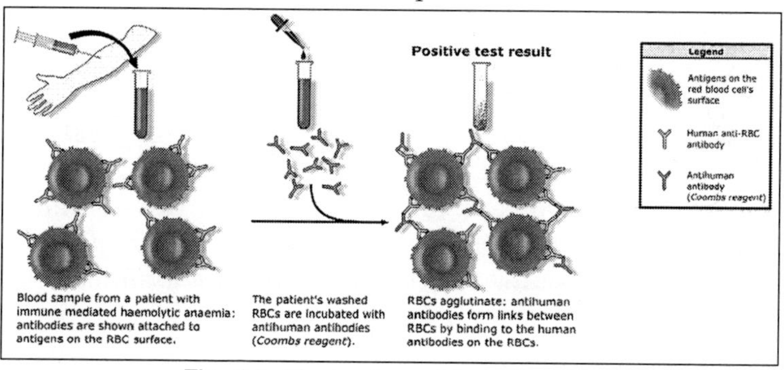

Fig. 4.1: Mechanism of Agglutination

MECHANISM OF CROSS-LINKING

The first in agglutination is the linking together of different particles or cells by antibody molecules that specifically attach to the antigenic determinants on the surface of the particles or cells. There is formation of large lattices through the cross-linking by the antibody molecules.

These lattices are generally visible with the naked eye as clumps. Multivalent IgM antibody is a more effective agglutinator of these relatively enormous cells than the IgG antibody.

MECHANISM OF SEDIMENTATION

Large lattices formed through cross-linking sediment readily due to the large size of the clumps. The force that causes the particles to sediment, for a given particle density, is proportional to the third power of its radius. On the other hand, the friction force, which counteracts sedimentation is proportional to the radius of the particles. Big particles will therefore sediment readily, whereas small particles are more strongly subjected to frictional forces that delay their sedimentation. Apart from their small size, another factor that may delay or even prevent sedimentation is the electrostatic repulsion between particles or cells having the same electric charge on their surface or "**Zeta Potential**".

VISUALIZATION OF AGGLUTINATION

Agglutination can be practiced in tubes or on slides and it can be visualized with the naked eye or under the microscope.

AGGLUTINATION IN TUBES

The method used in most agglutination tests is agglutination in tubes. For the titration of antibodies, a constant amount of antigen is added in a row of tubes containing serially diluted antiserum. After mixing and incubation at 37° C for 18 hours the tubes are examined for agglutination and agglutination is observed as clumps or flakes in a clear surrounding medium. The first few tubes which contain high amounts of antibody do not show agglutination, this is called the prozone phenomenon and this phenomenon can be explained on the basis of the fact that there are enough antibodies which can bind to all possible antigens on the surface independently with both their valences, instead of one antibody molecule linking two antigenic determinants on two neighboring particles and hence preventing the formation of a lattice. A similar phenomenon is the post zone non-agglutination which takes place in conditions of excess antigen because of similar reasons, that is, antibodies bind to the antigen but are not capable of cross-linking the particles. Between the two extremes, the cross-linking of antigen and antibody will generally give rise to three dimensional lattice structures which will coalesce to form large precipitating aggregates.

AGGLUTINATION ON SLIDES

This method has the advantages of being faster and of requiring smaller volumes of reagents than agglutination in tubes, this method is most frequently employed in ABO and Rh blood grouping. The procedure may be carried out on microscope slides, large glass plates, or white porcelain or plastic tiles. The drawback of the method is that it is less sensitive than the tube method, and is not suitable for quantitative work.

PRE-REQUISITES FOR AGGLUTINATION REACTION

(a) The antigen should be in particulate form.

(b) The antibody should be directed to the target antigen.

(c) Antigen and antibody should be present in optimal proportions.

(d) An electrolyte such as sodium chloride is necessary for the reaction to take place. Salt concentration and pH have significant effects on agglutination.

TYPES OF AGGLUTINATION

There are basically two types of Agglutination:

(a) **Direct Test:** Direct agglutination test diagnoses Ab against a large number of Ag like bacteria and fungi. The test is carried out in plastic micro titre plate with small wells, where each well acts like a small test tube. Each well contains equal amount of particular antigen but the amount of antibody is serially diluted and so, concentration is half in comparison to previous well. In a positive reaction, agglutination occurs and sufficient Ab are present in the serum to link the Ag together. However, in a negative test agglutination does not occur as insufficient antibodies are present for binding of Ag.

1. **Direct Haemagglutination:** The great bulk of blood grouping and cross-matching work is done by this method. ABO or Rh grouping is usually done on a slide by mixing a drop of test blood and a drop of specific antiserum (know as anti-A, anti-B or anti-Rh sera) with clean applicator sticks. The slide is tilted with a circular rolling motion and is observed for agglutination within a few minutes, appropriate controls are included in the test. Specific antisera are available commercially or can be prepared from a donor serum after selective absorption with red blood cells of a particular blood group. High titre antisera are used in the test. Titration of the antisera is done in the usual manner using whole blood or a 3% suspension of RBC in normal saline (Fig. 4.2).

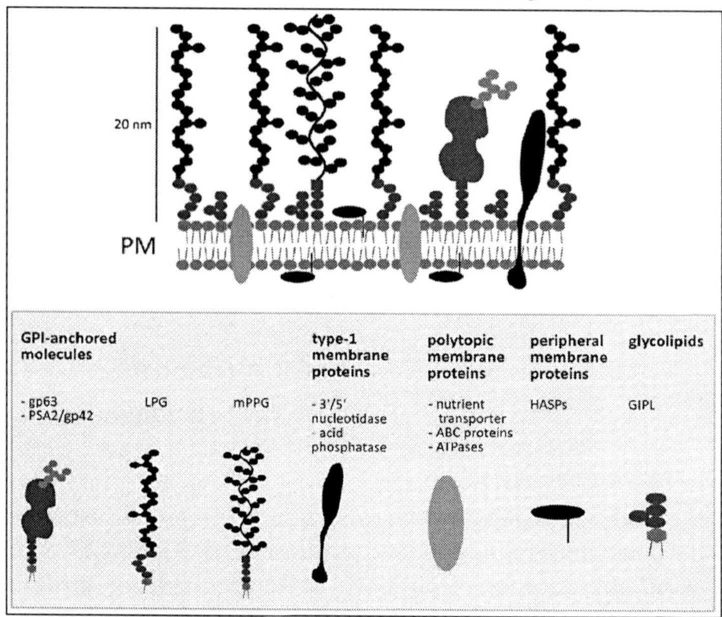

Fig. 4.2: Direct Agglutination

For the purpose of blood transfusion, donor and recipient blood samples have not only to be typed for compatibility of major groups like ABO, Rh and M, N etc., but also have to be mixed with each other to examine for any unknown or minor incompatibility. For this purpose, donor red cells are incubated with recipient serum and observed for agglutination.

2. **Anti globulin reaction (Coombs test):** In situations where Ig G-type antibodies bind to the given antigenic determinants on the red cell surface without causing visible agglutination, the indirect haemagglutination method is used to demonstrate the presence of those antibodies. Such antibodies are called 'non-agglutinating' or 'incomplete' antibodies. These antibodies can be demonstrated by using antiserum to lgG. This test is called the antiglobulin reaction or the "Coombs test" and two types of this test system are described below:

   (a) **Direct Coombs test:** This procedure is used to demonstrate that red cells taken directly from the circulation are already having 'non-agglutinating' or 'incomplete' antibodies bound on their surface. In this test patient's red cells are washed thrice with normal saline and then treated with rabbit anti-human antibodies (Coombs serum), which help in agglutinating the sensitized red cells (Fig. 4.3).

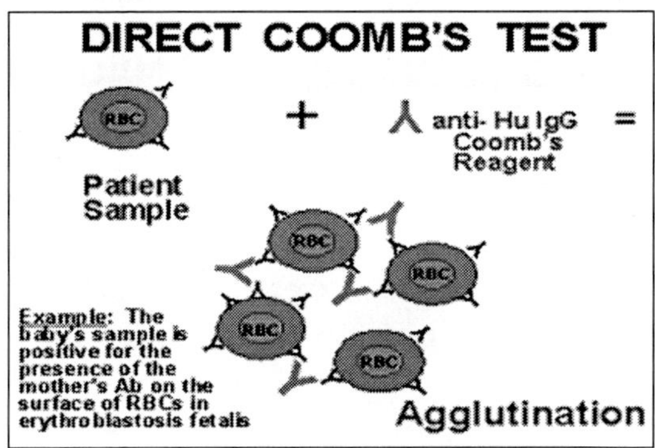

Fig. 4.3: Direct Coomb's Test

(b) **Indirect Coombs Test:** This procedure is used to test for the presence of 'non-agglutinating' antibodies against red blood cell antigens in patient's serum and the test is set up in a row of tubes. The test serum is serially diluted two folds in normal saline, washed sheep red blood cells (SRBC; 3%) are then added to all the tubes. Lastly Coombs serum (rabbit anti-human antibodies) is added to all tubes and the tubes examined for agglutinating. If non-agglutinating (incomplete) antibodies are present in the test serum, Coombs serum provides the second antibody to bring about agglutinating of red cells (Fig. 4.4).

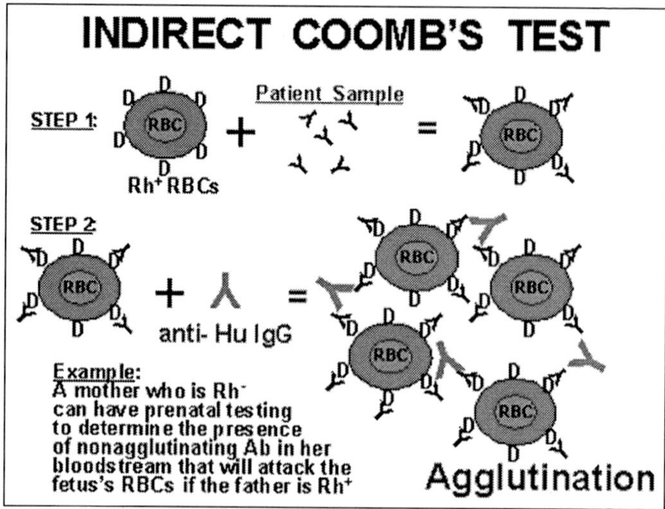

Fig. 4.4: Indirect Coomb's Test

Indirect Test: This is a very common test applied for detection of AMke *Streptococci* or other kinds of bacteria as antibodies react with soluble Ag by adhering to the particles. In this indirect test we detect the concentration of Ag and there are many types of haemagglutination, these include:

(a) **Passive Haemagglutination:** It is basically agglutinating of red cells by antibodies specifically directed to soluble antigens that have been previously adsorbed or otherwise attached to the red cell surface. Red cells are very popular as inert particles for various reasons. Erythrocytes of man, rabbit, chicken and sheep can be readily obtained in bulk amounts with little effort. These are particles of almost uniform size and shape. The most important feature of these particles is that they are red in colour and their agglutination is very easy to observe. It is for these reasons that these cells are most popular for use in agglutination reactions specially where a choice of inert particle is possible. Agglutination of red cells in a tube shows a typical pattern. The non-agglutinated cells settle to the bottom of the tube as a clear red 'button', while agglutinated cells settle as pink diffuse 'mat'. Since the visualization is so simple the test can also be carried out on microscale using micro-titer plate. This makes the test quick and suitable for application in the field where many samples have to be tested at a time and the presence of heterophile antibodies in the test serum may lead to false positive results. These antibodies can be removed prior to testing by absorption of the serum with red cells of the same batch that are not coated with the antigen.

(b) **Anti globulin Passive Haem Agglutination Test:** This procedure is similar to that described above for passive haem agglutination test (section) but an additional reagent (antiserum to IgG antibodies) is required to bring about agglutination of the red cells. The test is applicable in situations where 'non-agglutinating' or in complete' antibodies are present.

(c) **Haemagglutination Inhibition Test:** The amount of an antigen can be measured by the visible reactions of precipitation or direct agglutination with antibody. However, if this reaction is too weak, it can be measured by its capacity to inhibit the agglutination of antibody and the antigen bound onto some solid particles, like RBCs. This type of reactions are called haemagglutination inhibition assays and red cells are commonly used as the solid support for coating the antigen in these assays. The test can be carried out as usual by setting up a series of tubes (12 × 75 mm) or in a microhaemagglutination tray (v-shaped cups), containing decreasing amounts of the soluble antigen to be determined in 0.6 ml of saline 0.2 ml of antiserum, which contains excess antibody to give a good haemagglutination reaction with the red cell suspension which, is added to all tubes. The tubes are incubated after shaking at 37° C for 30 minutes and then 0.2 ml of 4% suspension of washed sensitized erythrocytes in saline is added after which the tubes are incubated again at 37° C for 1 hour. The reaction is read by observing the settling pattern of red cells. The last dilution of the antigen which inhibits agglutination represents the liter of the antigen (Fig. 4.5). In these assays It is very important to set up the following controls to rule out false negative and false positive results:

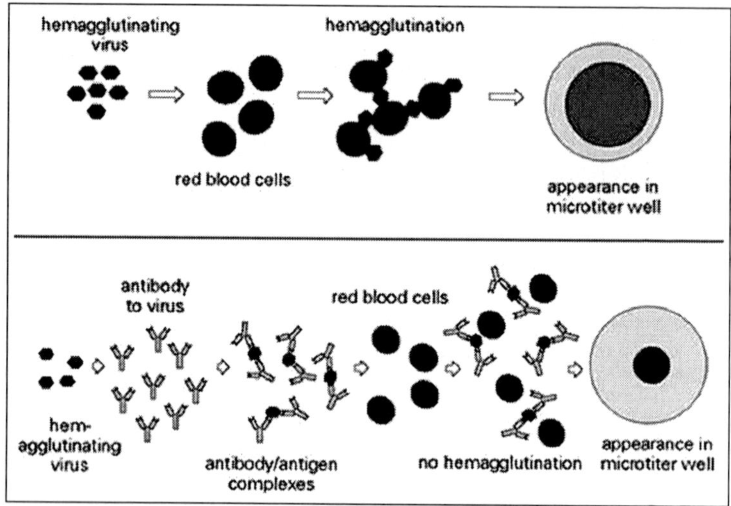

Fig. 4.5: Haemagglutination

1. **Antigen control:** Put a parallel series of tubes (till first four dilutions of the antigen as in the main series) which contain antigen sensitized cells but no antibody, to see if the antigen is non-specifically agglutinating the cells.
2. **Antibody control:** A tube containing only sensitized cells and antibody to check the spontaneous agglutination of the indicator system.
3. **Un-Sensitized Cells:** A control containing un-sensitized cells and antibody should not show any agglutination, the assay becomes valid only if these three controls are found to be satisfactory.

(d) **Mixed agglutination:** It refers to the formation of aggregates by agglutination of two different cell types or particles, brought about by antibodies that react with similar antigenic determinants on both types of cells. This is a technique for demonstrating the presence of specific cell surface antigens of one of the cell types with the help of second cell types (eg. red cells) carrying the known surface antigen as the indicator suspension (Fig. 4.6).

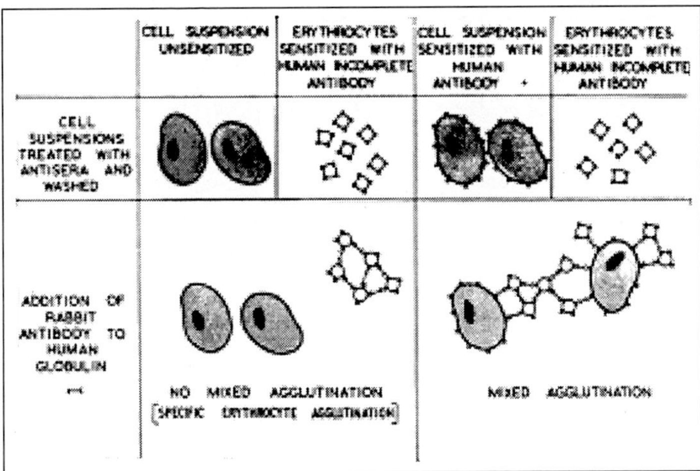

Fig. 4.6: Mixed Agglutination

(e) **Bacterial Agglutination:** It is the agglutination of bacteria as a test for the demonstration of the presence of anti-bacterial antibodies in sera was the oldest application of agglutination reaction. Many bacterial species, such as *Salmonella, Shigella, Preteus, E.coli, Gonococci* and *Meningococci* form smooth suspensions in buffered saline. When incubated with antibodies directed against surface antigens like those of flagella, capsular material or cell wall components, the bacteria agglutinate to form clumps or flakes. The bacterial suspension to be used should not subject to auto agglutination. Any antigens or other substances that may interface with specific agglutination should be removed, if present, by prior processing. Agglutination has formed the basis of widely used tests for identification and measurement of antibodies using known bacterial preparations. It is also used for identification of bacterial strains using specific antisera. These tests provide numerous diagnostic procedures and are a useful tool for immunological test (Fig. 4.7).

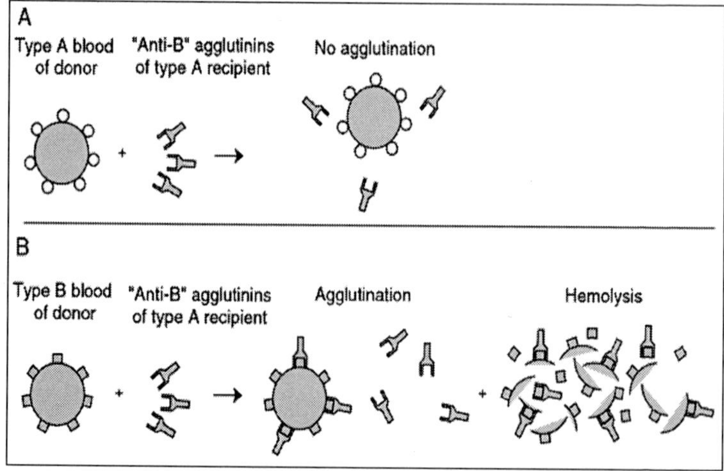

Fig. 4.7: Mixed Agglutination

Detection and Quantification of Antibodies by Bacterial Agglutination: Widal test is a serological test for the detection of antibodies directed against flagella ('H') and cell wall (somatic '0') antigens of *S. typhi* and *S. paratyphi* in patients suspected to be suffering from enteric fever (typhoid or paratyphoid fever). This can be discussed as a prototype of bacterial agglutination test.

The antigen used in Widal test is the whole bacteria which exposes either 'H' or 'O' antigen on the surface. The details of the methods of cultivation of bacteria, preparation of antigens from them and the quantitation of bacterial suspensions by Mc Farland's nephelometer are described elsewhere. The antiserum to be assayed should be clear of particles and lipid globules, although it is not necessary but in some cases inactivation of serum at 56° C improves the final reading of the test. The test is generally set up in tubes (12×75 mm). Serial two fold dilutions of antiserum from 1:5 to 1:640 is carried out in 0.5 ml of saline. Then 0.5 ml of an appropriate concentration of bacterial cell suspension adjusted to tube number 1 of Mc Farland's scale (18) is added to all tubes. The tubes are shaken and incubated at 37° C for 18 hours and are then held at 4° C for 2 hours before being read for agglutination, the reaction is observed against a light source. Agglutination is evidenced by presence of clumps visible after slight flicking of the tubes. 'O' agglutination is visible as fine granular clumps whereas 'H' agglutination is visible as large flasks. In tubes not showing agglutination the sediment bacterial rise like "**Smoke Puff**" on flicking of the tubes. The last dilution of the antiserum showing definite agglutination is taken as the titer of the serum. A control containing bacterial suspension and saline and another containing antisera (highest concentration) and saline should be put up alongside the above series of tubes to rule out false positive result. A standard positive serum control can be put up for comparison and for checking against false negative result. Widal type tests have also been successfully established for other infections like those caused by *Staphylococcus, Brucella abortus, Proteus, H.pertussis, Shigella, Pneumococcus, Mycobacteria, Francisella tularensis, Rickettsiae* and *Treponema.*

APPLICATIONS OF AGGLUTINATION

Agglutination test has varied number of application in clinical field, some of the applications of agglutination are following:

1. Agglutination reaction are used in ABO blood grouping system.
2. Agglutination reaction are also used in Rh blood grouping.
3. It is also applied in WIDAL and Well Felix test used for typhoid detection.
4. Coombs test for the identification of anti-Rh antibodies.
5. Brucella agglutination test is used for the detection of Brucella antibodies.
6. Leptospira agglutination test is also successfully implied for testing leptospirosis.
7. Cold agglutination test are also successfully implied for testing of malaria and trypanosomiasis.
8. Haemagglutination inhibition test is used for the diagnosis of certain viral and parasitic diseases.

POINT TO REMEMBER

1. Ag-Ab interact in such a way that they generate visible clumping, this reaction or clumping is referred as agglutination.
2. It is a highly sensitive reaction and the antibodies which produce agglutination are called "Agglutinins".
3. These agglutinins are capable of reacting with bacterial cells, white blood cells or RBC's as agglutination results in formation of flocculent masses or compact granules which are visible by naked eyes.

4. Agglutination occurs optimally when antibodies or agglutinins react with particulate antigen in equivalent proportion.
5. Agglutination reaction is one method to put in evidence of antigen antibody interaction where there is a specific antibody to an antigen present on surface of particles.
6. The reaction takes place as a result of particles coming together and producing a visible clumping (agglutination).
7. The particles can be bacteria, cells of higher plants or animals, micro fungi, or rickettsia.
8. Synthetic polymer particles like latex, bentonite and collodion can also be agglutinated after attachment of antigens on their surface.

QUESTIONS

1. What is agglutination, explain the basic concept of agglutination?
2. Explain the different types of agglutination?
3. Explain the mechanism of agglutination?
4. Explain the different applications of agglutination?
5. Explain in detail about haemagglutination?
6. Write a short note on bacterial agglutination?

Radioimmunoassay (RIA)

INTRODUCTION

Radioimmunoassay (RIA) is an immunological technique using radio active substances for quantitative measurement and identification of antigens (Ag), antibodies (Ab), hormones and drugs etc. This technique uses the competition between radiolabeled and unlabeled substances in an Ag-Ab reaction to determine the concentration of unlabeled substances. The technique involves use of radioisotopes instead of enzymes as labels to be conjugated with antigens or antibodies and the technique of detection of the antigen-antibody complex is called radioimmunoassay (RIA). Radioimmunoassay (RIA) may be define as an *in-vitro* assay that measures the presence of an antigen with very high sensitivity.

HISTORY

The technique was developed on 1960 by S.A. Berson and Rosalyn Yalow and Rosalyn R. Yalow who received the Nobel Prize for it in 1977, in the Veterans Administration Hospital in New York. It was the first assay technique to determine the presence of hormone level in blood using in-vitro assay.

PRINCIPLE OF RIA

The classical RIA methods are based on the principle of competitive binding and in this method, an unlabeled antigen competes with a radiolabeled antigen for binding to an antibody with the appropriate specificity. Thus, when mixtures of radiolabeled and unlabeled antigen are incubated with the corresponding antibody, the amount of free (not bound to antibody) radiolabeled antigen is directly proportional to the quantity of unlabeled antigen in the mixture (Fig. 5.1).

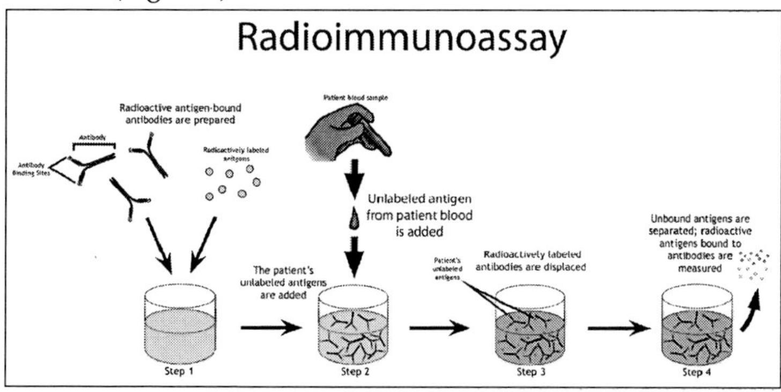

Fig. 5.1: Basic Principle of RIA

Process of RIA: It involves a combination of three principles (Fig.5.2).

1. An immune reaction which involves binding of antigen and antibody.
2. A competitive binding or competitive displacement reaction, which is required to give specificity.
3. Measurement of radio emission which gives sensitivity.

The process can be visualized in details as:

1. **Immune Reaction:** When a foreign biological substance enters into the body bloodstream through a non-oral route, the body recognizes the specific foreign substance as antigen and body produces specific antibodies against the antigen so as to neutralize the effects of Ag and to keep the body safe. The antibodies are produced by the

body's immune system so, it is an immune reaction. Here the antibodies or antigens move due to chemical influence which is different from principle of electrophoresis where proteins are separated due to charge.

2. **Competitive Binding or Competitive Displacement reaction:** This is a phenomenon wherein when there are two antigens that can bind to the same antibody, the antigen with more concentration binds extensively with the limited antibody displacing others. So here in the experiment, a radiolabeled antigen is allowed to bind to high-affinity antibody. Then when the patient serum is added unlabeled antigens in it start binding to the antibody displacing the labeled antigen.
3. **Measurement of Radio Emission:** Once the incubation is over, then washings are done to remove any unbound antigens. Then radio emission of the antigen-antibody complex is taken, the gamma rays from radiolabeled antigen are measured. The target antigen is labeled radioactively and bound to its specific antibodies (a limited and known amount of the specific antibody has to be added). A sample, for eg. blood-serum, is added in order to initiate a competitive reaction of the labeled antigens from the preparation, and the unlabeled antigens from the serum-sample, with the specific antibodies. The competition for the antibodies will release a certain amount of labeled antigen. This amount is proportional to the ratio of labeled to an unlabeled antigen. A binding curve can then be generated which allows the amount of antigen in the patient's serum to be derived. That means as the concentration of unlabeled antigen is increased, more of it binds to the antibody, displacing the labeled variant. The bound antigens are then separated from the unbound ones, and the radioactivity of the free antigens remaining in the supernatant is measured. Antigen-antibody complexes are precipitated either by

crosslinking with a second antibody or by means of the addition of reagents that promote the precipitation of antigen-antibody complexes. Counting radioactivity in the precipitates allows the determination of the amount of radiolabeled antigen precipitated with the antibody. A standard curve is constructed by plotting the percentage of antibody-bound radiolabeled antigen against known concentrations of a standardized unlabeled antigen, and the concentrations of antigen in patient samples are extrapolated from that curve.

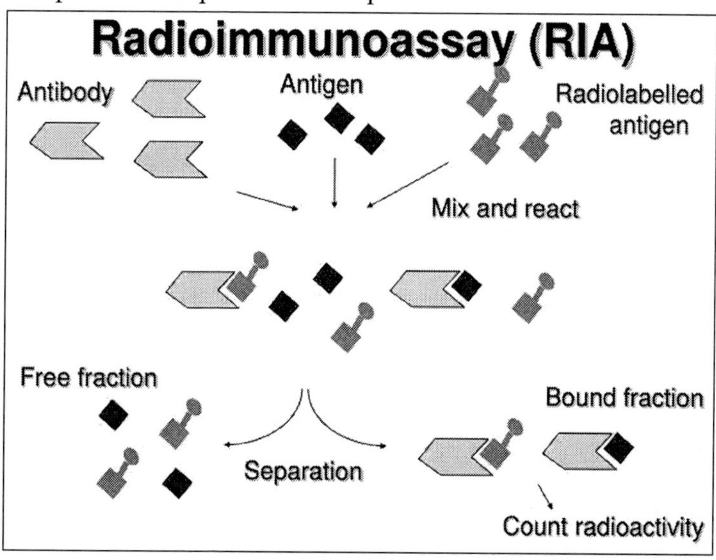

Fig. 5.2: Process of RIA

Steps in RIA: Technique of RIA involves following steps:

1. A limited known amount of a particular Ab is fixed on a solid phase.
2. A known and fixed level of Ag is labelled with radioactive iodine
3. The test sample containing unknown Ag and labelled Ag are mixed with Ab.

4. Labelled and unlabeled (test sample) Ag complete with each other for the Ab binding sites, the greater the amount of test Ag is present, lesser the labelled Ag will bind to the Ab.
5. The Ag-Ab complexes formed are separated and the amount of radio activity is determined.
6. As, the concentration of unlabeled Ag increases, the competition for binding to Ab also increases, resulting in lowering of the binding with labelled Ag consequently. reducing the radio-active count.
7. The concentration of unknown, unlabeled Ag is determined by comparison with reference standard (Fig. 5.3).

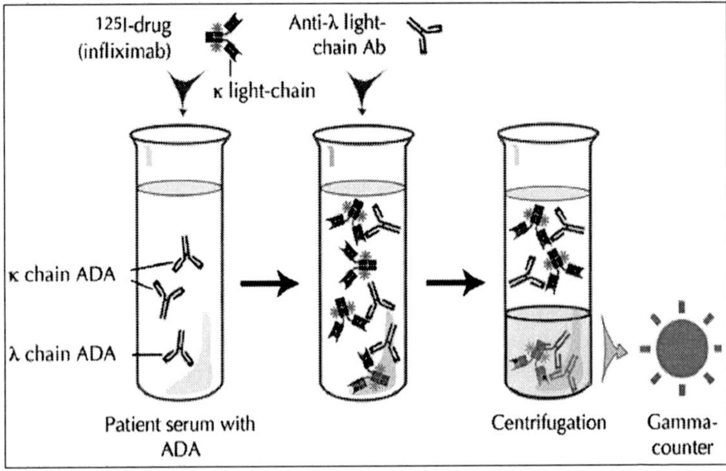

Fig. 5.3: Steps in the process of RIA

Calibration Curve: A standard curve can be constructed by plotting the percentage of antibody-bound radiolabeled antigen against known concentrations of a standardized unlabeled antigen as shown in figure. However, the curve allows determining the unknown antigen concentration directly from the standard curve.

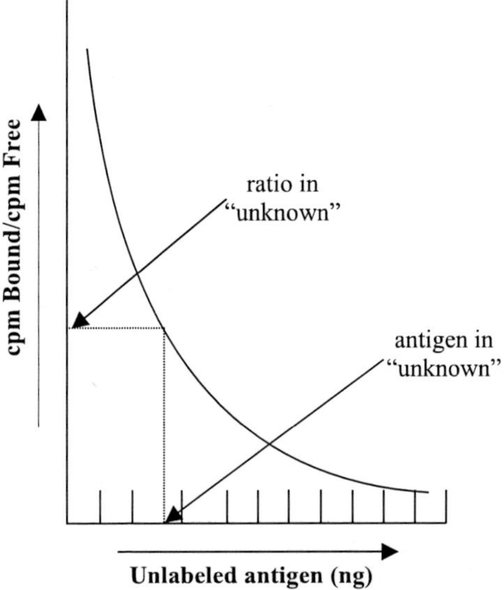

Fig. 5.4: Calibration Curve in RIA

APPLICATIONS OF RIA

Applications of RIA include following:

1. RIA is a sensitive technique, which permits measurement of Ag in very small quantities.
2. This technique is commonly used in reproductive biology and endocrinology for the assay of hormones in as small amount as picogram.
3. The technique is applied to detect Ig E, hepatitis B antigen, enzyme, serum proteins, drugs and vitamins.
4. The test can be used to determine very small quantities (e.g. nanogram) of antigens and antibodies in the serum.
5. The test is used for quantitation of hormones, drugs, HBs Ag, and other viral antigens.
6. RIA is used to analyze nano molar and picomolar concentrations of hormones in biological fluids, i.e. it allows detection in very small amount.

Limitations of RIA: There are some limitations of RIA which include following:

1. The cost of equipment and reagents
2. Short shelf-life of radio-labelled compounds.
3. The problems associated with the disposal of radioactive waste.
4. The process is a little unsafe and there are chances of hazards caused by it during preparation and handling the radioactive antigens.
5. The radiolabelled compounds have a short shell-life.
6. Requirements of special counter for radioisotopes makes the process little complicated.
7. There are problems associated with the disposal of radioactive waste, which makes the process little non-environment friendly.

POINTS TO REMEMBER

1. RIA is an immunological technique which uses the competition between radiolabeled and unlabeled substances in an Ag-Ab reaction to determine the concentration of unlabeled substances.
2. RIA is a sensitive technique used for the detection of antibody (Ab), Hepatitis B Ag, drugs and vitamins. It is also used for the detection of hormones.
3. The classical RIA methods are based on the principle of competitive binding. In this method, an unlabelled antigen competes with a radiolabelled antigen for binding to an antibody with the appropriate specificity.
4. Thus, when mixtures of radiolabelled and unlabelled antigen are incubated with the corresponding antibody, the amount of free (not bound to antibody) radiolabelled antigen is directly proportional to the quantity of unlabelled antigen in the mixture.

QUESTIONS

1. Explain the process of radioimmunoassay?
2. Explain the basic principle of RIA?
3. Explain the process of RIA?
4. Explain the different steps involved in RIA?
5. Explain the different applications of RIA?
6. Explain the different limitations of RIA?

Enzyme Linked Immunosorbent Assay (ELISA)

INTRODUCTION

Enzyme linked immunosorbent assay (ELISA) is an analytical biochemical assay first described by "Engvall and Perlmann" in 1971. The assay uses a solid phase type of enzyme immunoassay to detect the presence of a ligand (commonly a protein) in liquid sample using antibody (Ab) directed against the protein to be measured.

HISTORY

ELISA was pictured after the discovery of radioimmunoassay (RIA) by Yalow and Sussman. In 1971 "Engvall and Perlmann" discovered a technique known as "Enzyme linked immunosorbent Assay" ELISA.

PRINCIPAL OF ELISA

In ELISA specific substance is used for detection of antigen (Ag) or antibody (Ab). It is also used to detect or to separate component from mixture. In this process antigen (Ag) or antibody (Ab) is absorbed on the plate. After, this the sample from which Ag or Ab is to be detected is left on the plate. In the next step secondary linked Ab is added after which substrate is added. Finally, in the last step the change in the product is analyzed qualitatively and quantitatively by ELISA reader or spectrophotometer (Fig. 6.1).

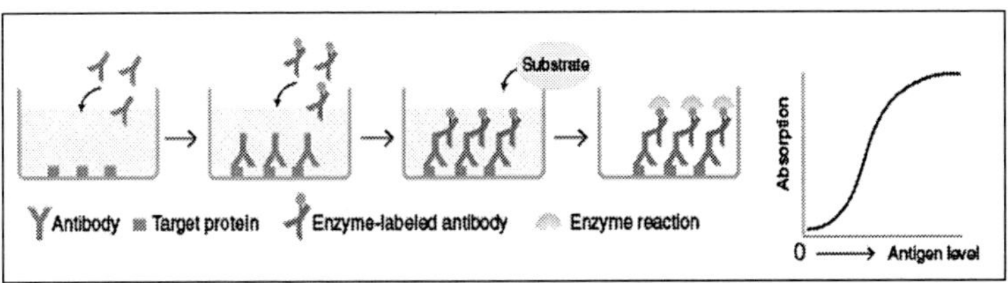

Fig. 6.1: Principle of ELISA

TYPES OF ELISA

ELISA is of basically of four types:

(a) Direct ELISA

(b) Sandwich ELISA

(c) Competitive ELISA

(d) Indirect ELISA

(a) **Direct ELISA**: The steps in the process of direct ELISA are following:

1. In the first step Ag to be tested is absorbed on the microliter plate and is left stable for some time.
2. After, this Bovine serum albumin (BSA) or casein is left on the plate so that the entire stretch of the plate is coated (even that also which is not covered with Ag) is coated with Ag.
3. Then, primary Ab attached with an enzyme is added to the well this then binds well to the test Ag.
4. After this, a substrate for this enzyme is added and this substrate changes color upon reacting with the enzyme.
5. The higher the concentration of the primary Ab present in serum, stronger is the color change. An ELISA reader or spectrophotometer is used to study the color change (Fig. 6.2).

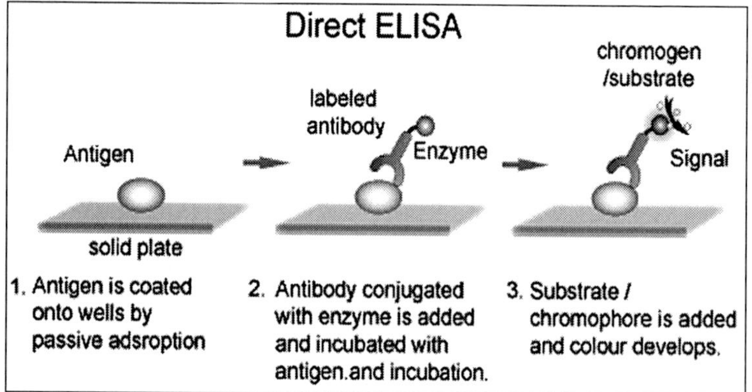

Fig. 6.2. Direct ELISA

(b) **Sandwich ELISA:** This method of ELISA is used to detect Ag present in the sample, following steps of ELISA are followed:

1. A surface is prepared to which known quantity of captured Ab is bound.
2. Any, non-specific binding sites on the surface are blocked.
3. The Ag containing sample is applied to the plate and is captured by Ab.
4. The plate is washed to remove unbound Ag.
5. A specific Ab is added which binds to the Ag, the primary Ab could also be in serum of a donor to be tested for reactivity towards Ag.
6. Then, enzyme linked secondary Ab is applied as this antibodies (Ab) bind specifically to antibody specific region.
7. The plate is washed to remove the unbound Ab conjugated with the enzyme.
8. A chemical/substrate is added which is converted by the enzyme into a color.
9. The color change is then estimated qualitatively and quantitatively by ELISA reader or spectrophotometer.

10. As, Ag is sandwiched between two antibodies so, this ELISA is known as "Sandwich ELISA" (Fig. 6.3).

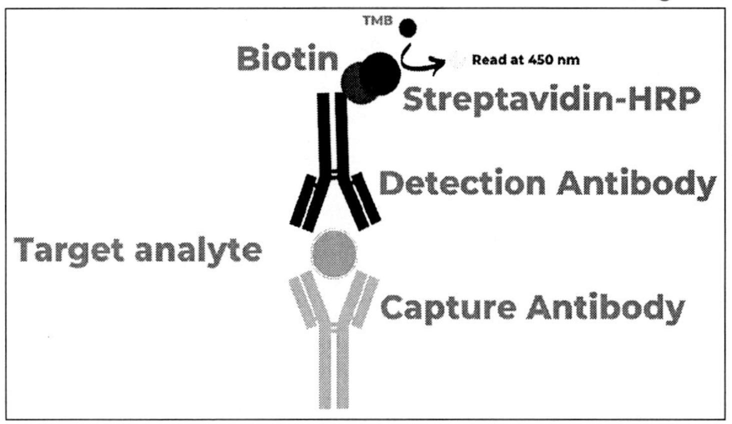

Fig. 6.3: Sandwich ELISA

(c) **Competitive ELISA**: In this ELISA following steps are followed:

1. Unlabeled Ag is incubated in the presence of its Ag and these bound Ag-Ab complexes are added to an Ag coated well.
2. After, this the plate is washed, so that the unbound Ab's are removed.
3. The secondary Ab coupled to enzyme and specific to primary Ab is added to the plate.
4. A substrate is added and enzyme elicits a color change.
5. The color change is then qualitatively and quantitatively estimated with ELISA reader or spectrophotometer (Fig. 6.4).

(d) **Indirect ELISA**: Indirect ELISA follows the following steps:

1. Indirect ELISA is done with variety of modifications to basic ELISA.
2. Ag of choice is bound to the experimental surface.

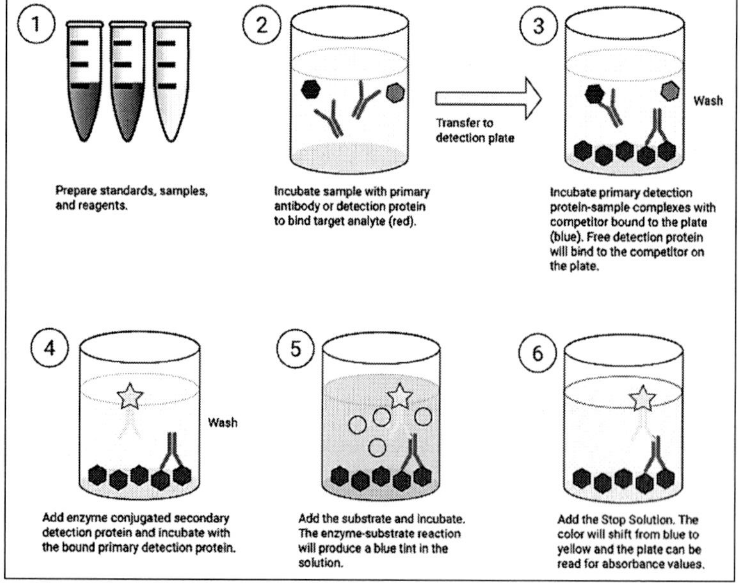

Fig. 6.4: Competitive ELISA

3. An unlabeled primary Ab specific for it is added and it binds to the primary Ab.
4. Since, the secondary Ab can be directed against more than one primary Ab.
5. A colorless substrate is introduced to the sample, which reacts with the enzyme conjugate and produces a measurable by-product.
6. Depending on the choice of substrate, the by product can be either measured by colorimetric, ELISA reader or spectrophotometer (Fig. 6.5).

(d) **Applications of ELISA**

Following are the applications of ELISA:

1. ELISA is used to estimate Ag/Ab count in the given sample.
2. ELISA is used to analyze allergy arising due to food stuff etc.

3. ELISA is used to estimate serum Ab concentration in a given sample.
4. ELISA is used in the detection of diseases like HIV and HBV.
5. It is also used to detect diseases in dogs, cattle and other animals.
6. ELISA is also applied in food industries for testing food allergens present in the sample.
7. ELISA is also used in toxicology as rapid preventive screen for certain class of drugs.
8. ELISA is also used for the detection for many complicated diseases like AIDS, Hepatitis and COVID.

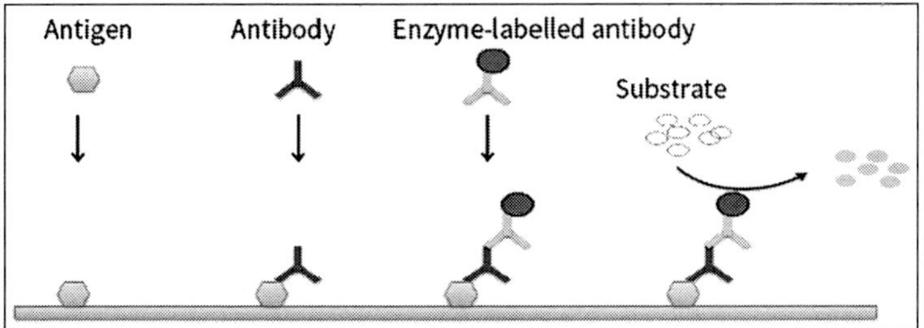

Fig. 6.5: Indirect ELSIA

POINTS TO REMEMBER

1. In ELISA specific substance is used for detection of antigen (Ag) or antibody (Ab).
2. ELISA is used to detect or to separate component from mixture, in this process antigen (Ag) or antibody (Ab) is absorbed on the plate.
3. After, this the sample from which Ag or Ab is to be detected is left on the plate.
4. In, the next step secondary linked Ab is added after which substrate is added.
5. Finally, in the last step the change in the product is analysed qualitatively and quantitatively by ELISA reader or spectrophotometer.

6. There are basically four types of ELISA viz. Direct ELISA, Sandwich ELISA Indirect ELISA and Competitive ELISA.

QUESTIONS

1. Explain the basic principle of ELISA?
2. Explain the basic process of ELISA?
3. Explain about different types of ELISA?
4. Explain the mechanism of ELISA?
5. Explain the different applications of ELISA?

Monoclonal Antibodies (MAb)

INTRODUCTION

The body naturally produces antibodies, which are elements of the immune system produced by B-lymphocytes, these are capable of binding with foreign proteins in the body known as antigens, which aims at eliminating them out of the body. They are found naturally circulating in the body searching for foreign bodies (antigens) where they attach once to the antigen; they destroy the antigen using various immune mechanisms. On, the other hand, monoclonal antibodies are proteins prepared in the laboratory to target specific antigens on body cells such as receptors and other foreign proteins on the surface of normal and cancer cells in the body.

Monoclonal antibodies are artificial antibodies that are produced from a single clone of cells by fusing B-lymphocytes to myeloma cells. The fusion of B-lymphocytes with myeloma cells by somatic cell hybridization secrete desired antibody-producing elements which are immortalized cell-lines known as a hybridoma and these hybridomas produce homogenous monoclonal antibodies.

Monoclonal antibodies (M Abs) have the ability to recognize unique binding sites (epitopes) found on the specific antigens. This differentiates monoclonal antibodies from polyclonal antibodies i.e monoclonal antibodies are derived from a single B-cell clone to target single epitopes, unlike polyclonal antibodies that target multiple epitopes. Monoclonal antibodies (M Abs) have been produced to target receptors or other foreign proteins that are present on the surface of normal cells and cancer cells. Monoclonal antibodies are used in the treatment of many diseases including some cancers. The specificity of monoclonal antibodies (MAbs) allows them to bind to cancerous cells coupled with a cytotoxic agent such as a strong radioactive agent. The radioactive agent seeks to destroy the cancer cells without harming the healthy ones.

TYPES OF MONOCLONAL ANTIBODIES

Being synthetically manufactured to act like human antibodies in the immune system, monoclonal antibodies are prepared in 3 different ways and they are named after what they are made of:

1. **Murine Monoclonal Antibodies:** They were the first monoclonal antibodies to be produced on a lab-scale by the hybridoma technology in 1975. They were named murine because of their origin from rodent hosts (mice and rats) belonging to the *Muridae* family. The murine M Abs have played a crucial role in the development of modern antibody production techniques and the potential applications of these artificial immunoglobulins in therapeutics and analytical applications. In therapeutic applications, they are used as a framework for the development of antibody and engineering techniques that include chimerization, humanization, and development of bispecific antibodies from antibody fragments known as single-chain antibody fragments (scFvs). Preclinical trials to use murine M Abs on the capsular polysaccharide and enhance the therapeutic activity of amphotericin B administration, the name of their treatments ends with –omab.

2. **Chimeric Antibodies:** These are structural chimeras that are made of a combination of mouse parts, human parts or by fusion. This involves fusing variable regions of one species such as mice and the constant regions of the other species such as the human species. Chimeric monoclonal antibodies are produced to reduce immunogenicity and to increase the serum half-life when preparing them for therapeutic reasons. Chimeric antibodies retain the original antibody's antigen specificity and affinity and the name of their treatments ends with -ximab.
3. **Humanized Monoclonal Antibodies:** They are an extension of the chimeric monoclonal antibodies where by, all regions of the mouse antibody in chimeric M Abs are replaced with human ones except for the complementarity-determining regions (CDRs) which are the amino acids that make direct contact with the antigen. This means that humanized M Abs have small parts of the mouse protein that are attached to the human protein. The names of treatments end in -zumab. Monoclonal antibodies can also be classified based on the functions they play, such as monoclonal antibodies used in cancer treatment include:
   (a) **Naked Monoclonal Antibodies:** These are M Abs these do not have a drug or radioactive agent attached to them, these are the most commonly used in the treatment of cancer. Most naked M Abs attach to the antigens on the cancer cells and others bind to antigens or other non-cancerous cells or free-floating proteins. These naked M Abs function differently for example they boost immune response against the cancer cells by attaching to the cancer cells and act as markers for the body's immune systems to destroy them eg. Alemtuzumab which is (Campath) used for treating chronic lymphocytic leukaemia (CLL). This drug Alemtuzumab binds to the CD_{52} antigen

found on the lymphocytes including leukemic cells, there by attracting immune cells to them thus by destroying them and boosting the immune response by targeting the immune system checkpoints. Attaching to and blocking the antigens on cancer cells that facilitate growth and spread of cancer cells and other neighbouring cells eg. trastuzumab (Herceptin) is a M Ab designed against HER2 protein of breast and stomach cancer and blocks their activation, this HER2 protein facilitates the growth of the cancer cells.

(b) **Conjugated Monoclonal Antibody:** These are also known as labelled/tagged or loaded antibodies, which are conjugated MAbs and are combined with chemotherapy drugs or a radioactive agent. They are mainly used as homing devices in driving the chemotherapy drug directly to the cancer cells. Conjugated MAbs circulate freely throughout the body until it finds and attaches (hooks) onto the target antigen and delivers the antigen to immune elimination processes. The advantage of conjugated monoclonal antibodies is that they reduce the risks of damaging normal cells in other body parts.

(c) **Radiolabeled Monoclonal Antibody:** They possess a small radioactive particle attached to them where the drug along with radioactive agents are delivered directly to the target cells, causing the traditions to affect the target and the neighboring cells to some extent. For example, *Ibritumomab tiuxetan (Zevalin)* acts against CD_{20} antigen found on the B-lymphocytes. They deliver the radioactivity directly to the cancer cells. Ibritumomab tiuxetan drugs are made up of MAb drugs known as *rituximab.*

PRINCIPLE FOR PRODUCTION OF MAb

The basic principle involved in the production of Mab is the fusion of myeloma cell with B cell to form hybridoma using polyethylene glycol as agent. Three different hybrids are formed viz. B-B, B-Mylenoma and Mylenoma-Mylenoma. Out of these three hybrids the hybrid which is fusion of B-Mylenoma will survive as it will gain property of long life from mylenoma cell and property of antibody production from B cell. Hybrid cells are used for monoclonal antibody production either in in-vivo or in in-vitro conditions and before starting the process of Ab production the mice is primed with pristine after which the hybrid cells are transferred. The monoclonal antibodies are produced in the acetic fluid or peritoneal cavity of mice which gives production of about 1-25 mg/ml of Mab. This mode of production is preferred over production in flask because production in flask does not give that much of count (Fig. 7.1).

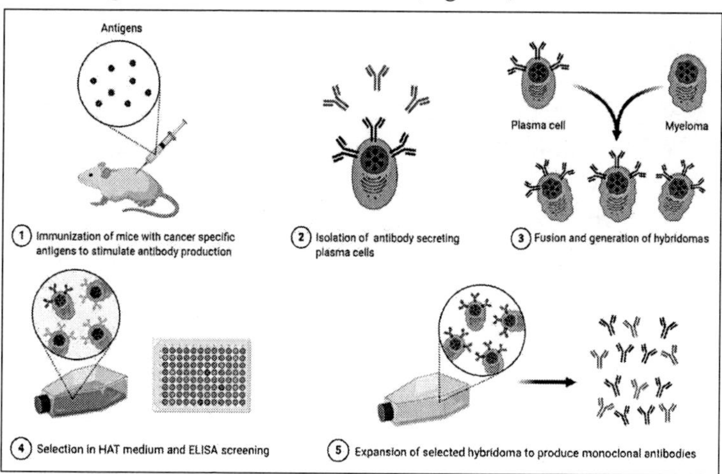

Fig. 7.1: Principle of Monoclonal Antibody Production

PRODUCTION OF MAb

Hybridoma technology was first discovered by G. Kohler and C. Milstein during 1975 to produce a hybrid cell. These hybrid cells are produced by fusing B-lymphocyte with tumor cell and they are called as myeloma cells. Thus, these hybrid cells have got the ability to produce antibody (Ab) due to B-lymphocyte genetic material and also capacity to divide indefinitely in culture due to the presence of tumor or myeloma cells involved in the production of hybrid cells. Therefore, these hybrid cells which are produced from hybridoma technology are cultured in laboratory or sub-cultured using mouse peritoneal cavity and this technology is called as hybridoma technology, the production of monoclonal antibodies takes place in following steps:

1. **Immunization:** B-lymphocytes are extracted from the spleen of an animal, but usually it is extracted from the mouse, which has been immunized with the required antigen (Ag) against which MAb are produced. Mouse is immunized by giving Ag injection along with adjuvant via subcutaneously or by peritoneal cavity, this is followed by booster doses of the Ag. The immunization with specific Ag increases the specific antibody producing B-lymphocytes, this considerably increases the chances of obtaining required hybridoma cells or clones.
2. **Cell Fusion:** The specific Ab producing lymphocyte are then mixed with selected myeloma cells and are induced to form hybrid cells. The myeloma cells are selected based on some criteria like these cells themselves should not produce Ab and also they should contain a genetic marker such as HGPRT. This genetic marker helps in easy selection of resulting cells. When HGPRT myeloma cells are fused with specific Ab producing B-lymphocytes, the resulting cell population will have the mixture of cell population such as hybrid cells, myeloma cells, B-lymphocytes.
3. **Selection of Hybridomas:** This mixture of cell population is then cultured in selective media known as HAT medium in which, only the hybridoma cells grow, while the rest will slowly disappear. This happens

in 7-10 days of culture and selection of a single Ab producing hybrid cell is very important which is possible if the hybridoma are isolated and grown individually. The suspension of hybridoma cells is so diluted that the individual aliquots contain on an average one cell each. When these cells grow in a regular culture medium the produce the desired Ab. Actually, selection in the HAT medium depends on two ways of nucleotide synthesis, these include:

(a) **Denovo Pathway:** The De novo pathway requires synthesis of nucleotides by phosphoribosyle and uridylate, but the presence of aminopterin blocks this pathway thus, stopping the synthesis of nucleotides. Due to the presence of aminopterin the De novo pathway is blocked and the cells utilize salvage pathway for nucleotide synthesis.

(b) **Salvage Pathway:** When the De novo pathway is blocked the cells utilize Salvage pathway for nucleotide synthesis. This pathway uses HGPRT and thymidine kinase enzymes and the presence of HAT medium allows the action of these enzymes, allowing the growth of nucleotides on HAT medium in Salvage pathway (Fig. 7.2).

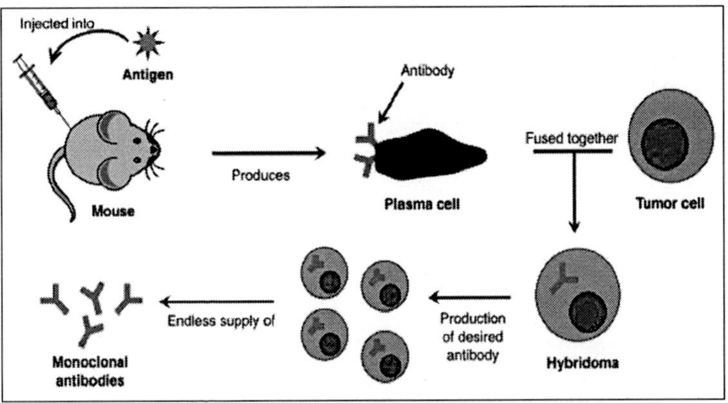

Fig. 7.2: Production of Monoclonal Antibody

APPLICATIONS OF MONOCLONAL ANTIBODY

M Ab has many applications in different medical fields, some of the important applications include following:

1. **Diagnostic Applications:** M Ab are utilized in diagnostic kits for the diagnosis of various infectious diseases, detecting pregnancy, diabetes, cancer and monitoring drug levels, matching histocompatibility antigen etc.
2. **Therapeutic Applications:** Graft-versus host disease (GVHD) is a major cause of mortality and morbidity after allogenic bone marrow transplantation, but can be avoided by removing T-lymphocyte from donor bone marrow. However, T-cell depletion increases the risk of graft rejection and the study examined ensures that CD_{52} MAb can eliminate T-cells from both donor marrow and recipient to prevent GVHD and Alemtuzumab M Ab is used for this propose.
3. **In the treatment of cancer:** M Ab are useful for the treatment of cancer and the antibody (Ab) bind to cancer to destroy them. This is brought about antibody dependent cell mediated cytotoxicity, complement mediated cytotoxicity and phagocytosis of cancer cells by reticuloendothelial system. A monoclonal antibody specific to the cells of leukemia is used to destroy the residual leukemia cells without affecting other cells. M Ab is used in vivo to remove the residual tumor cells prior to autologous bone marrow transplant.
4. **Treatment for allergic diseases:** Most of the allergic disease are caused by Ig E mediated hypersensitive reactions. M Ab is used for the detection of Ig E and monoclonal antibody is also used successfully for the treatment of many known allergic diseases.
5. **In dissociation of blood clots:** The blockage of arteries occurs due to inadequate dissolution of blood clots. Tissue Plasminogen Activator (tPA) can be used as a therapeutic agent to remove blood clots.

6. **In Drug Delivery:** The sufficient quality of the drug does not reach the target tissue, tissue specific M Ab can solve this problem. The drug can be coupled with MAb and can reach specific target cell or site of action.
7. **In Radio Immunotherapy:** The radioisotopes can be coupled to MAb that are directed against tumor cells. This allows the concentration of radioactivity at the desired sites and a very efficient killing of target cells (tumor cells). The advantage with radio immunotherapy is that conjugated complex need not penetrate the cells., as it is required in immunotoxin therapy.
8. **Vaccine Production:** Many vaccines like antimalarial vaccines have been prepared by using M Ab, which specifically include the production of malarial vaccines which can inhibit the multiplication of Plasmodium against malarian parasite.
9. **Monoclonal Antibodies as Enzymes:** Use of M Ab as enzyme is very common in the field of biotechnology as these M Ab can bind with specific ligands.
10. **M Ab in the purification and quantification of molecules:** These antibodies are used widely for purification and quantification of certain molecules like hormone and cyclic nucleotide. These are also used for detecting small volume of body fluids and antigens in the body.
11. **Study of cellular mechanism and hormone production:** M Ab is used to detect T and B cells because these cells have their own markers and M Ab is produced against the markers itself. M Ab are also used for isolation and production of certain important hormones like interferon (Fig. 7.3).

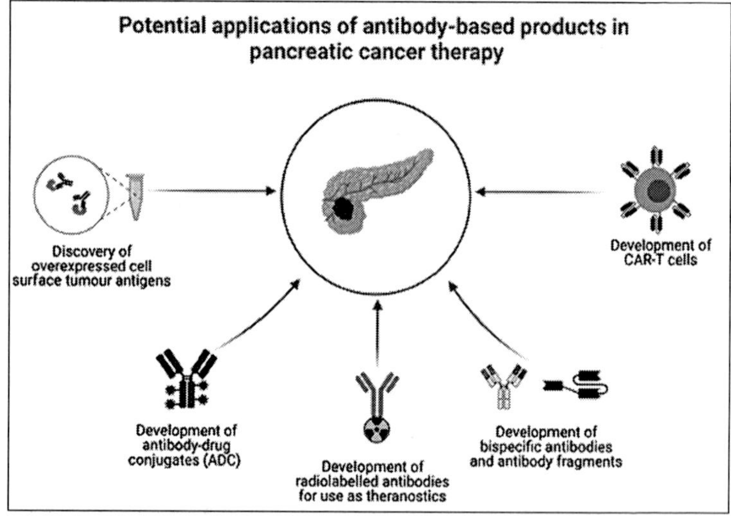

Fig. 7.3: Applications of Monoclonal Antibodies

POINTS TO REMEMBER

1. MAb are the antibodies synthesized against single antigenic determinant and are produced by hybridoma technology.
2. The basic principle involved in the production of Mab involves the fusion of myeloma cell with B cell to form hybridoma using polyethylene glycol as agent.
3. Three different hybrids are formed viz. B-B, B-Mylenoma and Mylenoma-Mylenoma.
4. Out of these three hybrids the hybrid which is fusion of B-Mylenoma will survive as it will gain property of long life from Mylenoma cell and property of antibody production from B cell.
5. Hybrid cells are used for monoclonal antibody production either in in-vivo or in in-vitro conditions. Before starting the process of Ab production the mice is primed with pristine after which the hybrid cells are transferred. The monoclonal antibodies are produced in the acetic fluid or peritoneal cavity of mice which gives production of about 1-25 mg/ml of Mab.

6. This mode of production is preferred over production in flask because production in flask does not give that much of count.
7. M Ab is used for the disease diagnosis, disease treatment, therapeutic applications, enzymes vaccine production and cancer treatment.

QUESTIONS

1. Explain in detail about Monoclonal Antibodies?
2. Explain the process of Monoclonal Antibody Production?
3. Write a short note on De novo pathway and Salvage Pathway?
4. Explain in brief about the principle of Monoclonal antibodies?
5. Explain in detail about the applications of Monoclonal antibodies?

Diagnostic Techniques of COVID

INTRODUCTION

Diagnostics has been a crucial aspect in COVID-19 pandemic as three major methods for the detection of SARS-CoV-2 infection/COVID virus and their role has evolved during the course of the pandemic. Molecular tests such as PCR are highly sensitive and specific at detecting viral RNA, and are recommended by WHO for confirming diagnosis in individuals who are symptomatic and for activating public health measures. Some other test like antigen rapid detection test which detects viral proteins, carry the advantage of being easier and simpler, are known to give faster result, have lower cost, and are able to detect infection in those who are most likely to be at risk of transmitting the virus to others are commonly used for COVID detection. Antigen rapid detection tests can be used as a public health tool for screening individuals at enhanced risk of infection, it also protects people who are clinically vulnerable to disease and also ensures safe travel and resumption of schooling and social activities which enables economic recovery. With vaccine roll-out, antibody tests can be useful surveillance tools to inform public policy, but should not be used to provide proof of immunity, as the correlates of protection remain unclear. All three types of COVID-19 test continue to have a crucial role in the transition from pandemic response to pandemic control.

DIAGNOSTIC TECHNIQUES OF COVID

An unprecedented number of novel diagnostic tests have been developed for COVID-19 using new technologies. Three types of diagnostic tests are relevant to patient management and pandemic control, they include Rapid Antigen Test, RT-PCR and Omicure Kit which can detect viral RNA antigen and viral proteins (eg. nucleo capsid or spike proteins). At, the same time different serology tests that detect host antibodies in response to infection, or vaccination, or both are frequently used. The first two types of tests can be used to diagnose acute infection. By contrast, serology tests provide only indirect evidence of infection 1-2 weeks after the onset of symptoms and are best used for surveillance. Until there is better understanding of the correlates of protection, clinical indications for serologic testing in health-care settings are inadequate. Some of the common diagnostic techniques used in diagnosis of COVID are following:

1. **Rapid Antigen Test:** The COVID-19 Antigen self-test is a single-use, in vitro (outside the body) visually read rapid immunoassay that usually uses a human nasal swab specimen for the qualitative detection of nucleo capsid protein SARS-CoV-2 antigen (Ag). The COVID-19 Antigen Self-Test is intended to be used manually by untrained lay users (self testing) in a private setting to aid in the diagnosis of an active SARS-CoV-2 infection. The novel coronaviruses belong to the β genus and COVID-19 is an acute respiratory infectious disease where people are generally susceptible to lung infections. Currently, the patients infected by the novel coronavirus are the main source of infections, asymptomatic infected people can also be an infectious

source. Based on the current epidemiological investigation, the incubation period is 1 to 14 days, mostly 3 to 7 days. The main manifestations include fever, fatigue and dry cough, nasal congestion, runny nose, sore throat, myalgia and diarrhoea are found in a few cases.

PRINCIPLE

The COVID-19 antigen self-test is a lateral flow test that detects the nucleo capsid protein antigen of the Coronavirus SARS-CoV-2 in a swab from the mid turbinate nasal region. The product includes a test device, a bottle with buffer solution, an extraction tube/cap and a nasal swab. To use the test, buffer solution is added to the extraction tube, then a human nasal specimen is collected using the swab provided in the kit. After sample collection, the nasal swab is transferred to the extraction tube to extract the Coronavirus proteins. Then, next, 5 drops of extracted sample are applied to the round well on the test device. A line in the Control (C) line area within the result reading window will only become visible if the test was performed correctly. A line in the Test (T) line area within the result reading window will only become visible if Coronavirus proteins are detected. The presence of only one Control (C) line, without visible Test (T) line, indicates the coronavirus proteins are not present. Active ingredients of the test device are antibodies specific to the SARS-CoV-2 nucleo capsid protein antigen.

KIT CONTENT

The kit includes following:

Test 1—— Instructions for Use, 1 Test Device, 1 Tube, 1 Blue Cap, 1 Buffer Bottle, 1 Swab, 1 Bag, 1 Tube Rack.

4 Tests—— 1 Instructions for Use, 4 Test Devices, 4 Tubes, 4 Blue Caps, 4 Buffer Bottles, 4 Swabs, 4 Bags, 1 Tube Rack.

10 Tests—— 1 Instructions for Use, 10 Test Devices, 10 Tubes, 10 Blue Caps, 10 Buffer Bottles, 10 Swabs, 10 Bags, 1 Tube Rack.

20 Tests—— 1 Instructions for Use, 20 Test Devices, 20 Tubes, 20 Blue Caps, 20 Buffer Bottles, 20 Swabs, 20 Bags, 2 Tube Racks.

STORAGE AND STABILITY

For storing the kit following should be kept in mind:

1. Store the test kit in a cool, dry place (at 2-30° C). Do not freeze the kit or its components.
2. Do not use the test kit beyond the expiration date as indicated on the outer package.
3. Perform the test immediately after removing the Test Device from the protective packaging.
4. Do not store the test kit in direct sunlight.

PROCEDURE FOR TEST

The test is accomplished in following steps:

1. **Preparation of the Test:** Before, the test following points should be checked:
   (a) Check the expiry date on the box and the test kit should not be used if it is expired.
   (b) Ensure that the kit is at room temperature for at least 30 minutes prior to use.
   (c) The box should be opened and each component should be removed, the individual components should not be opened until instructed.
   (d) Keep Buffer Bottle upright, twist and pull tab to open bottle.
   (e) Squeeze the liquid from the Buffer Bottle into the Tube. You will need to squeeze at least twice.
2. **Collection of Nasal Samples:** The sample should be collected in following manner:
   (a) Open Swab protective package at stick end, take Swab out.

(b) Insert the soft end of the Swab straight back into your nostril until resistance is felt (about 2cm). Slowly rotate the Swab, gently rubbing it along the insides of your nasal passage at least 5 times. Remove Swab from nostril, it is better if both nostrils are swapped together.

(c) Using the same Swab, repeat step 7 in your other nostril.

(d) Insert the Swab into the Tube and swirl in the fluid 5 or more times while pushing against the wall of the Tube. Pinch the Swab tip through the Tube to remove any remaining fluid.

(e) Hold the Tube firmly with one hand, lift the Swab and locate the break line and snap the Swab handle at the break line (Fig. 8.1).

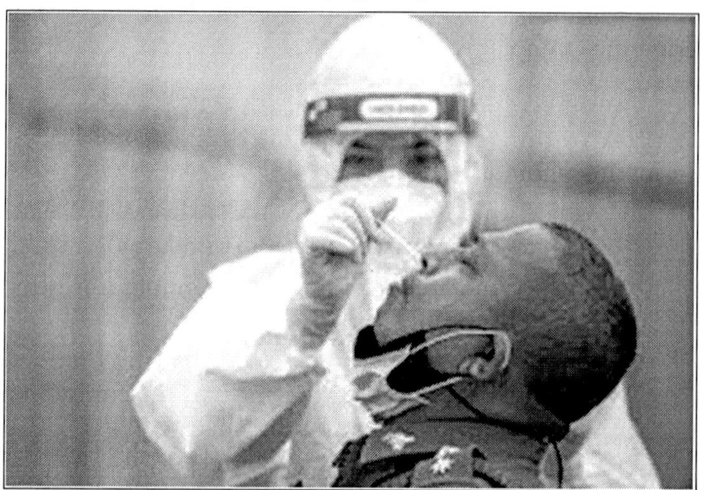

Fig. 8.1: Collection of Sample

3. **Perform the Test:** The test should be performed in following manner:

   (a) Remove the test device from its protective package and place on a well-lit, flat surface.

(b) Check liquid for bubbles and wait for any bubbles to disappear as they can lead to inaccurate results. The tubes should be kept in vertical with the white cap pointed down. Remove the white cap.

(c) Squeeze 5 drops of liquid from the Tube into the well on the Test Device. Secure white cap back on tube and wait for 15 minutes.

(d) Keep Test Device flat on table. After 15 minutes, use the NAVICA app to take a photo of the Test Device and submit your result.

(e) The app will automatically submit your result to ICMR and display your test result. Do not read the result earlier than 15 minutes or after 20 minutes.

(f) A Control (C) line may appear in the result window within a few minutes but a Test (T) line may take as long as 15 minutes to appear. After 20 minutes the result might become inaccurate (Fig. 8.2).

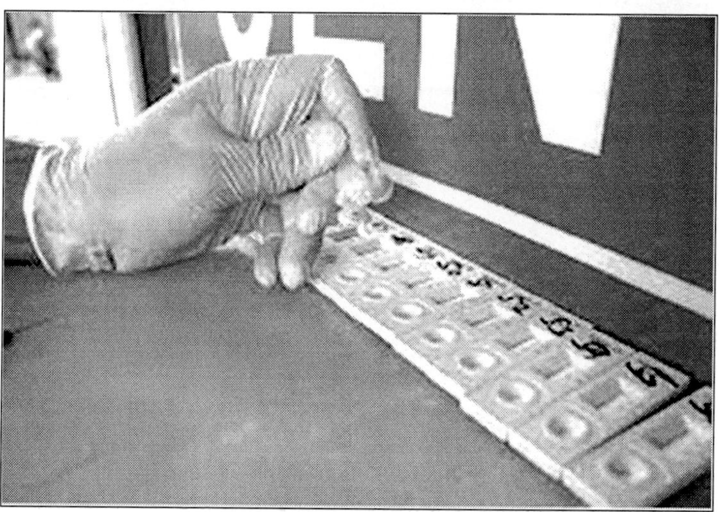

Fig. 8.2: Test Procedure

4. **Interpretation of the Result:** Three type of result can be interpreted:

   (a) **Invalid Results:** Find the result window and if NO Control (C) line is present, the test did not work and is considered Invalid. This may be the result of an incorrect test procedure and the test should be repeated.

   (b) **Positive Result:** Find result window and look carefully for two lines, if you see two lines, Control (C) line and Test (T) line, this means COVID-19 was detected positive.

   (c) **Negative Results:** Find result window and look for a single line in window. Negative Result: If you see only the Control (C) line is present, this means COVID-19 was detected negative (Fig. 8.3).

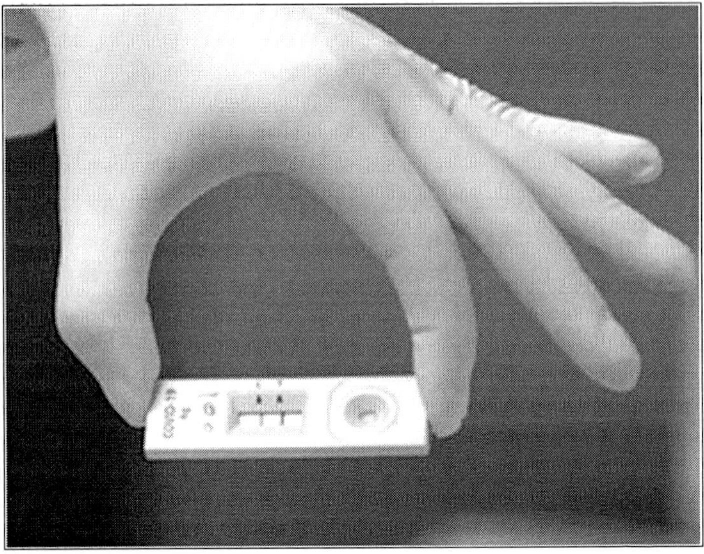

Fig. 8.3: Interpretation of the Result

5. **Kit Disposal:** After, performing the test the test kit should be disposed:

   (a) Place Swab, Tube and Test Device into the Bag.

(b) Seal the Bag tightly.

(c) Throw away the Bag in waste bin.

6. **Precautions:** Following precautions should be taken:

(a) For in vitro diagnostic use only.

(b) Read instructions prior to performing the test. Follow all instructions to achieve accurate results.

(c) Do not eat or smoke while handling specimens.

(d) Wash hands thoroughly before and after the test is completed.

(e) Clean up spills thoroughly using an appropriate disinfectant.

(f) Dispose of all specimens, reaction kits and potentially contaminated materials (i.e. Swab, Tube, Test Device) in bag provided.

(g) Use only the liquid from the Buffer Bottle provided in the kit. Use of other liquids will lead to inaccurate results.

(h) Keep the test kit out of reach of children.

(i) To prevent contamination, only touch the sides of the test Device and ensure the Swab end only touches the nasal cavity and inside of Tube.

(j) The provided Swab should be used only for nasal (mid-turbinate) specimen collection.

(k) Each single Test Device, Swab, Tube, Blue Cap, Buffer Bottle and Bag are single use, do not reuse individual components and the Tube Rack is reusable.

(l) Do not dip the Swab into buffer or other liquid before inserting the Swab into the nose.

2. **Real Time-Polymerase Chain Reaction (RT-PCR):** The COVID-19 detection by RT-PCR requires a detection Kit which is intended for the qualitative detection of nucleic acid from the SARS-CoV-2 in upper and lower

respiratory specimens (such as anterior nasal swabs, mid-turbinate nasal swabs, nasopharyngeal swabs, oropharyngeal swabs, sputum, lower respiratory tract aspirates, broncho-alveolar lavage, and nasopharyngeal wash/aspirate or nasal aspirate) from individuals suspected of COVID-19 by their healthcare provider. Results are for the identification of SARS-CoV-2 RNA and the SARS-CoV-2 RNA is generally detectable in upper and lower respiratory specimens during the acute phase of infection. Positive results are indicative of the presence of SARS-CoV-2 RNA, clinical correlation with patient history and other diagnostic information which is necessary to determine patient infective status. The agent detected may not be the definite cause of disease and positive results do not rule out bacterial co-infection with other viruses. Negative results do not preclude SARS-CoV-2 infection and should not be used as the sole basis for patient management decisions. Negative results must be combined with clinical observations, patient history, and epidemiological information. The COVID-19 RT-PCR Detection Kit is intended for use by qualified trained clinical laboratory personnel specifically instructed and trained in the techniques of real-time PCR and in vitro diagnostic procedures.

3. **Principle of Detection:** This product is a fluorescent probe-based Taqman RT-PCR assay system. Firstly, the RNA of SARS-CoV-2 will be reverse transcribed into cDNA by reverse transcriptase, and then PCR amplification will be performed with cDNA as template. During amplification of the template, the TaqMan probe will be degraded due to the 5′-3′ polymerase activity and exonuclease activity of Taq DNA polymerase, then the separation of fluorescent reporter and quencher enables the fluorescent signal to be detected by instrument. The ORF1ab gene of SARS-CoV-2 will be detected qualitatively by FAM channel, the N gene of SARS-CoV-2 will be detected, qualitatively by JOE

channel, the E gene of SARS-CoV-2 will be detected qualitatively by ROX channel, and the internal reference will be detected by CY5 channel. dUTP and UNG enzyme are used in the kit to prevent contamination of the amplified products. Internal reference is used in the kit for quality control starting from sample collection.

PRODUCT COMPONENTS

The COVID-19 RT-PCR Detection Kit includes the following components:

- SARS-COV-2 Reaction Reagent
- RT-PCR Enzyme
- Positive Control of SARS-CoV-2
- Negative Control
- Internal Reference A
- Sample collection from nasopharyngeal or oropharyngeal swabs or collection tubes or sputum containers.
- RNase/DNase free water, anhydrous ethanol
- 96 well plates, pipette tips with filters, micro-centrifuge tubes
- Liquid waste container, solid waste bag and container
- Double-layer latex gloves, waterproof boot covers, protective clothing, goggles, and masks with higher filtration efficiency.
- Applied Bio-systems 7500 instrument (software version #v1.4 or v1.5)
- PCR hood, centrifuge with rotor for 1.5 mL and 2 mL tubes, vortex mixer, metal bath, and pipette.

Storage and Shell-Life: All reagents should be stored at -25° C to -15° C (-13° F to 5° F) with protection from light, and the reagents are stable for 12 months when stored at the recommended condition and the expiry date of the kit should checked. The kit should be transported by cold chain transport or sealed foam box with ice. The temperature should be controlled below -8° C and the transportation time should not exceed 4 days.

Sample Collection: Sample collection should be conducted by qualified health care providers:

1. **Oropharyngeal swab (throat swab):** Wipe the bilateral pharyngeal tonsils and the posterior pharyngeal wall at the same time, immerse the swab head into the sample collection tube containing transport media, discard the tail, and tighten the tube cover.
2. **Nasopharyngeal swab:** Hold the nasopharyngeal swab close to the nasal septum slowly and deeply to the back of the nasopharynx, rotate it several times to obtain secretions; quickly dip the swab into the sample collection tube containing transport media, discard the tail, and tighten the tube cap to seal to avoid drying.
3. **Sputum:** Cough up the sputum in the deep part of the respiratory tract and collect it in the container. Liquefying method: add equal volume of acetyl cysteine (10 g/L) into the sputum sample, shake at room temperature for 30 minutes, and then carry out RNA extraction after sufficient liquefying.
4. **Temperature:** The sample can be stored at 2° C to 8° C for 24 hours, at -20° C for 4 days, and below -70° C for an extended time.
5. **Transport:** Samples shall be transported at low temperature in accordance with biosafety regulations.

Procedure of the Test: Reagent Preparation 7 Prepare reagent with ice box, and prepare reaction reagent according to the number of reaction samples (number of reaction samples, n = number of samples to be tested + 2 control samples, following steps should be followed:

1. **Mixing:** Add n × 6 μl of RT-PCR enzyme and n × 14 μl of SARS-CoV-2 reaction reagent into the centrifuge tube, mix by shaking, and centrifugate at low speed for a few seconds, then make aliquots of 20 μl into different PCR reaction tubes. The reaction tubes can be placed at 2° C to 8° C for 3 hours after separation.

2. **RNA Extraction:** It is recommended to use Q lamp Viral RNA Mini Kit (QIAGEN®) to extract RNA from samples and reference. The volume of sample to be extracted is 200 µl, and 5 µl of internal reference A will be added to each sample (including the reference); the RNA elution volume is 60 µL; after RNA extraction, the extracted RNA shall be added to the reaction tubes within 10 minutes, or transferred to the centrifuge tubes and stored at -25° C to -15° C.
3. **Template Addition:** Add 10 µL of extracted Negative Control, 10 µl of extracted Positive Control, and 10 µl of extracted RNA from sample to different PCR reaction tubes. Centrifuge them at low speed. Then, move them to the Real-time PCR instrument.
4. **PCR Amplification**: Following steps are followed:

   Step 1: 50°C for 15 minutes, 1 cycle;

   Step 2: 95°C for 3 minutes, 1 cycle;

   Step 3: 95°C for 5 seconds to 60°C for 40 seconds, 5 cycles;

   Step 4: 95°C for 5 seconds to 60°C for 40 seconds, 40 cycles. The signals of FAM, JOE, ROX and CY5 fluorescence channels will be collected at 60°C.
5. **Data Analysis:** Applied Bio system (7500RT-PCR software v1.4, v1.5) and test data file need to be saved after PCR reaction.
6. **Parameter Setting:** Please set the parameters and analysis the results of FAM, JOE, ROX and CY5 channels respectively:
   (a) **Baseline setting:** The baseline can be set automatically or adjusted according to the shape of amplification curve.
   (b) **Threshold setting:** The threshold value should be higher than the highest fluorescence value of negative control in this kit (Fig. 8.5).

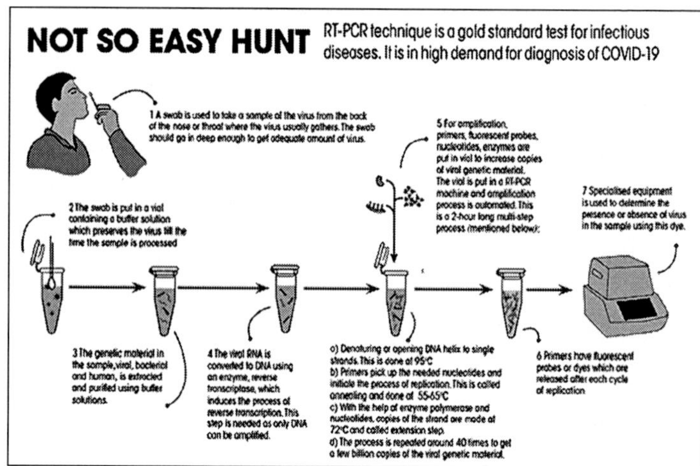

Fig. 8.4: Steps in RT-PCR

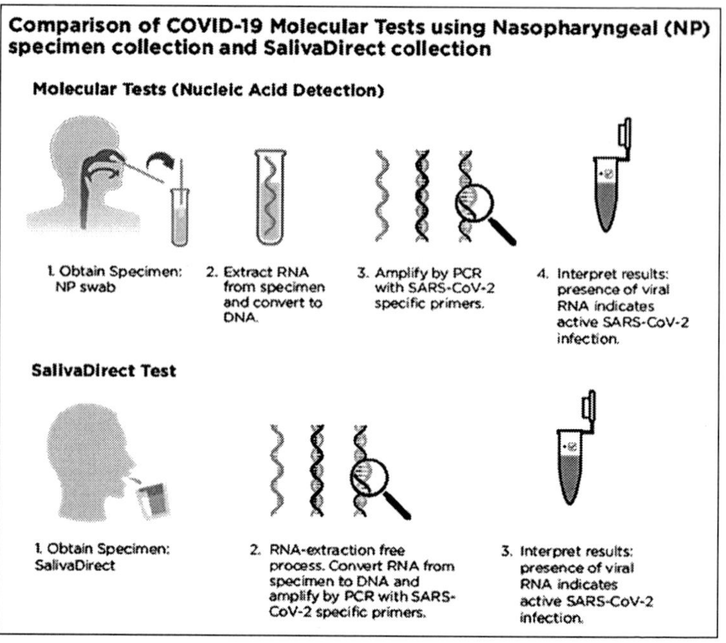

Fig. 8.5: Procedure of RT-PCR

7. **Quality Control:** Negative and positive control provide the calibration for the kit, and shall be set for each test. The result is valid if ALL the below criteria is met. Otherwise, the test is invalid. In this case, the errors of instruments, reagents, amplification conditions, etc. shall be checked, and the experiment shall be repeated (Table 8.1).

Table. 8.1: Quality Control Criteria

Product of Quality Control	Requirements of Quality Control			
	FAM Channel	JOE Channel	ROX Channel	CY5 Channel
Positive Control of SARS-COV-2	Ct ≤ 32	Ct ≤ 32	Ct ≤ 32	No requirement
Negative Control	Under	Under	Under	Ct ≤ 32

8. **Result Interpretation:** The results are interpreted as following:
   (a) FAM has amplification signal, Ct ≤ 36, and amplification curve is typical S shape, then ORF1ab gene (+); otherwise, ORF1ab gene (-).
   (b) JOE has amplification signal, Ct ≤ 36, and amplification curve is typical S shape, then N gene (+); otherwise, N gene (-).
   (c) ROX has amplification signal, Ct ≤ 36, and amplification curve is typical S shape, then E gene (+); otherwise, E gene (-).
   (d) If the Ct of FAM, JOE and ROX is more than 36 or no value; and the Ct of CY5 is more than 32 or no value, then there is a problem with the sample or operation, which needs to be retested (Table 8.2).

Table. 8.2: Criteria for Interpretation of Results

Test Results	IC Results	Interpreting Test Results
ORF1ab gene (+), N gene (+), E gene (+); OR ORF1ab gene (+), N gene (+), E gene (-); OR ORF1ab gene (+), N gene (-), E gene (+); OR ORF1ab gene (-), N gene (+), E gene (+)	(+) or (-)	2019-nCoV (+)
Only ORF1ab gene (+)	(+) or (-)	Test again, and if repeated: 2019-nCoV (+)
Only N gene (+) or E gene (+)	(+) or (-)	2019-nCoV (-)
ORF1ab gene (-), N gene (-), E gene (-)	(+)	2019-nCoV (-)
ORF1ab gene (-), N gene (-), E gene (-)	(-)	Test again

Cut Off Value: The cut-off value of COVID-19 is Ct ≤ 36.

LIMITATION

1. The performance of the COVID-19 RT-PCR detection kit was established using pharyngeal swab samples and sputum samples which may not be accurate.
2. Anterior nasal swabs and mid-turbinate nasal swabs are also considered acceptable specimen types for use with the COVID-19 RT-PCR Detection Kit but performance has not been established. Testing of nasal and mid-turbinate nasal swabs (self-collected or collected by a healthcare provider) is limited to patients with symptoms of COVID-19. Please refer to FDA's FAQs on Diagnostic Testing for SARS-CoV-2 for additional information.
3. Samples must be collected, transported, and stored using appropriate procedures and conditions, improper collection, transport, or storage of specimens may hinder the ability of the assay to detect the target sequences.
4. Extraction and amplification of nucleic acid from clinical samples must be performed according the specified methods listed in this procedure. Other extraction kits have not been evaluated.
5. The positive result detected by this kit can't indicate whether there is virus in vivo. It is suggested to use other methods for confirmation at the same time.
6. This kit is intended for classification and detection of SARS-CoV-2. The result is only for clinical reference, and the clinical management of patients should be considered in combination with their symptoms/signs, history, other laboratory tests and treatment responses.
7. Negative results do not preclude SARS-CoV-2 infection and should not be used as the sole basis for treatment or other patient management decisions. Optimum specimen types and timing for peak viral levels during infections caused by SARS-CoV-2 have not been determined.

Omisure Kit: Omisure kit can differentiate the omicron strain of the novel coronavirus from the delta, alpha and the other variants in under four hours. It is an omicron detecting RT-PCR kit developed by the Mumbai-based Tata Medical and Diagnostics Ltd (TATA MD) in partnership with the Indian Council of Medical Research (ICMR). The kit recently received approval from the Drugs Controller General of India. Omisure can be a game changer for detecting and controlling the Omicron variant because it can diagnose this variant in a single step.

Working of Omisure Kit: This new kit can identify the Omicron variant by targeting two regions of the S or the spike gene. This gene codes for the spike protein, which helps the novel coronavirus to enter and infect human cells. The S, the Enveloped (E), and Nucleo capsid (N) genes are some of the targets of conventional RT-PCR tests. When it detects these genes, a patient sample is labelled positive. As omicron bears heavy mutations in the S gene, the RT-PCR can sometimes miss it. The absence of S gene likely indicates omicron's presence. This is called S gene dropout or S gene target failure and is one of the targets of Omisure. This kit also depends on a second target: S gene mutation amplification, which detects mutations explicitly in the S gene. Despite being considered the gold standard, sequencing has a few limitations. It is slow, expensive and complicated. It is a multi-step process and it begins with extracting the virus' RNA from patient samples, converting it into DNA, amplifying or multiplying it through RT-PCR before finally sending it for gene sequencing. Globally, all other test kits for omicron are either made for gene dropout or mutation-specific detection.

Comparison of Genome Sequencing by Omisure Kit: Gene sequencing reads the order of nucleotides, which are the building blocks of deoxyribonucleic acid (DNA) and ribonucleic acid (RNA). denitrifying variants through gene sequencing can take as many as three days. Omisure, on the other hand, will do test the Omicron variant in four hours. Gene sequencing is also complicated and expensive as it has to be done in batches of 24, 96 or 384. Testing 384 samples on one sequencing chip "costs around Rs. 10,000 per sample. The cost is higher when the number of samples is lower and a single kit of Omisure will reportedly cost Rs. 250 for the laboratory.

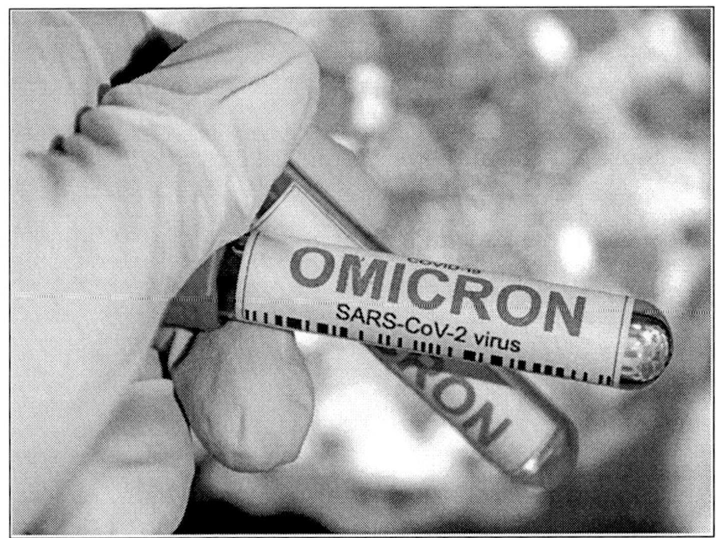

Fig. 8.6: Omicron Kit

POINT TO REMEMBER

1. An unprecedented number of novel diagnostic tests have been developed for COVID-19 using new technologies.
2. Three types of diagnostic tests are relevant to patient management and pandemic control, they include Rapid Antigen Test, RT-PCR and Omicure Kit which can detect viral RNA antigen and viral proteins.
3. At, the same time different serology tests that detect host antibodies in response to infection, or vaccination, or both areused for COVID detection.
4. The first two types of tests can be used to diagnose acute infection, by contrast, serology tests provide only

indirect evidence of infection 1-2 weeks after the onset of symptoms and are best used for surveillance.

5. Until there is better understanding of the correlates of protection, clinical indications for serologic testing in health-care settings are inadequate.

QUESTIONS

1. Explain the different diagnostic techniques of COVID?
2. Explain in detail about RT-PCR technique used for COVID detection?
3. Explain in detail about Rapid Detection kit?
4. Write a short note on Omisure kit?
5. Explain the principle of different diagnostic techniques used in COVID?

Immunobiotechnology

INTRODUCTION

When Immunology combines with biotechnology to be used for diagnosis and for treating different diseases it is termed as Immunotechnology. Immunotechnology is also involved in facilitating advanced research in immunology to decipher mechanisms under disease progression, establishment and identification of novel therapeutic targets. Immunobiotechnological techniques include Production of Humanized Antibody, Antibody Engineering using Genetic Manipulation, Recombinant Protein, Western blot, Northern Blot, Southern Blot and Immuno PCR. Immunology has applications in numerous medical disciplines, particularly in the fields of organ transplantation, oncology, rheumatology, virology, bacteriology, parasitology, and dermatology. Immunology is also fundamental to the life sciences industry, the discipline is core to the development of modern antibody therapies, cellular therapies, small molecule drugs, vaccines and 'biologics' (therapeutic biomolecules). Thus, combination of immunology and biotechnology aids in the generation of many techniques and immunoassay which are helpful for medical and diagnostic purposes.

HUMANIZED ANTIBODIES

A type of antibody made in the laboratory by combining a human antibody with a small part of a mouse or rat monoclonal antibody. The mouse or rat part of the antibody binds to the target antigen, and the human part makes it less likely to be destroyed by the body's immune system, the early success of mouse monoclonal antibodies led to the U.S. Food and Drug. Approval of the first therapeutic antibody OKT3 (Murom nab) in 1986, as a treatment for kidney transplant rejection was a landmark in development of humanized antibodies. However, most mouse antibodies were shown to have limited use as therapeutic agents because of a short serum half-life, an inability to trigger human effector functions and in particular they were recognized by the patient's immune systems as foreign proteins resulting in human anti-mouse antibodies (HAMA).

Humanized antibodies are antibodies from non-human species whose protein sequences have been modified to increase their similarity to antibody variants produced naturally in humans. The process is usually applied to monoclonal antibodies developed for administration to humans (for example, antibodies developed as anti-cancer drugs). Humanization can be necessary when the process of developing a specific antibody involves generation in a non-human immune system (such as that in mice). The protein sequences of antibodies produced in this way are partially distinct from homologous antibodies occurring naturally in humans and are therefore potentially immunogenic when administered to human patients. The International Nonproprietary names of humanized antibodies end in -zumab as in omalizumab. Humanized antibodies are distinct from chimeric antibodies and the latter also have their protein sequences made more similar to human antibodies, but carry a larger stretch of non-human protein.

Humanization is important for reducing the immunogenicity of monoclonal antibodies derived from xenogeneic sources (commonly rodents) and for improving their activation of the human immune system. Since the development of the hybridoma technology, a large number of rodent monoclonal antibodies with specificity for antigens of therapeutic interest have been generated and characterized. Rodent antibodies are highly immunogenic in humans, which limits their clinical applications, especially when repeated administration is required. Importantly, they are rapidly removed from circulation and can cause systemic inflammatory effects as well. As a means of circumventing these problems, three antibody have been developed which use humanization strategies that can preserve the specificity and affinity of the antibody toward the antigen while significantly or completely eliminating the immunogenicity of the antibody in humans. The first approach is CDR grafting and the second is chain shuffling. These two methods are all based on phage display of humanized sc Fv variants and selection of high-affinity humanized binders through bio-panning. The third method, humanized IgG library screening, is somehow unique. A library of humanized whole IgG to be displayed on the surface of mammalian cells is synthesized and then high-affinity binders will be sorted by FACS.

CDR Grafting and SDR Grafting: A CDR (complementarity-determining region) grafting platform, which is featured with randomization of a small set of framework residues using phage display technology and computer modelling is created. In this platform, six CDR loops comprising the antigen-binding site are grafted into corresponding human framework regions. Unfortunately, simple grafting of the rodent CDRs into human frameworks does not always reconstitute the binding affinity and specificity of the original antibody because framework residues are involved in antigen binding, either indirectly, by supporting the conformation of the CDR loops, or directly, by contacting the antigen. For this reason, we have developed a computer modeling method to randomize certain framework residues in addition to CDR grafting. The grafted CDRs together with the randomized residues are cloned into a phage display library and the humanized antibodies with the best affinity are selected by screening of the library. This approach allows the epitope specificity of the original antibody to be retained of note, humanization by this approach is not 100% since the CDR regions are still of a rodent origin. To reduce the immunogenicity of CDR-grafted humanized antibodies, the murine content in the CDR-grafted humanized antibodies is minimized through SDR grafting. Within each CDR, there are more variable positions that are directly involved in the interaction with antigen, i.e., specificity-determining residues (SDRs), whereas there are more conserved residues that maintain the conformations of CDRs loops. SDRs may be identified from the 3D structure of the antigen antibody complex and/or the mutational analysis of the CDRs. An SDR-grafted humanized antibody is constructed by grafting the SDRs and the residues maintaining the conformations of the CDRs onto human template, and its immunogenic potential is evaluated by measuring the reactivity to the sera from patients who had been immunized with the parental antibody.

Chain Shuffling: A chain shuffling strategy that is an entirely selective humanization strategy based on the construction and screening of two chimeric phage display libraries. In this approach, the light chain of the rodent antibody is first replaced by light chains in one of our well-tested human antibody libraries the resulting hybrid antibody library is then screened by panning against the particular antigen. After that, the heavy chain of the selected hybrid antibodies is replaced by the heavy chains of the human antibody library. Subsequent screening of this secondary chimeric library will produce fully humanized antibodies. Since phage display library screening mimics in vivo antibody selection and evolution procedure, chain shuffling can result in humanized antibodies whose affinities are higher than that of the original antibody. Also, this sequential chain shuffling procedure can generate several versions of humanized antibodies with different sequences. The production of multiple humanized antibodies retaining the same epitope specificity is important in therapeutic regimens that call for long-term treatment with antibodies in which anti-idiotypic responses might be avoided by the administration of alternative antibodies. The method based on chimeric phage display library construction and screening allows full, i.e. 100% humanization of a mouse antibody. A Phage Display Naive Human sc Fv Library with a complexity of 1.42×109 trans formants as the backbone of the chimeric libraries and the donor of human V L and V H chains can be constructed.

Humanized IgG Library Screening: In this method, a mammalian cell surface display library is made to display full-size humanized IgG variants that are further selected using FACS. First, an acceptor of human V_H and a receptor V_L from a sub group of human antibodies based on consensus sequences is selected. After this, CDR grafting is conducted in order to increase the affinity of the humanized antibodies, a mammalian cell surface display IgG library is created to display all possible variants of the humanized IgG. Since, the size limit for the mammalian cell surface displays the IgG library, decisions must be made as to which amino acids to diversify and to what extent so that there are fewer nonsense antibody mutants that waste the capacity of the library. Back mutations in framework regions are designed based on computer modelling or antigen/antibody structure information and there is a clear distinguish between residues with solvent-accessible side chains from those with buried side chains. We have confirmed that the randomization of residues with buried side chains is a waste of library sequence space. No mutation between glycine and tryptophan is observed since changes in these residues usually abolish binding. Sometimes, we study the AA sequence of the parent antibody to find out conserved framework positions. We may then introduce mutations to the positions in the framework regions that are not conserved. Supposedly, these regions will be antigen-specific and changes in these regions may increase affinity but not immunogenicity. In order to create the largest possible library, trimer codon technology is employed to randomize those defined framework residues on both humanized heavy-chain and humanized light-chain. Finally, the humanized IgG library is created, in which the cDNA of the heavy chain variants are cloned into a mammalian cell surface display vector, while the cDNA of the light chain variants are inserted into a separate mammalian expression vector to be expressed as free (not membrane-anchored proteins). The cDNA of the heavy-chain library and the light-chain library is then mixed and transfected into 293 cells for surface display of functional whole-size humanized IgG variants, top binders are then sorted by FACS. After stringent selections, a fraction of ELISA-positive mutant binders will have a higher affinity than the parent antibody. The affinity of the positive clones will be ranked using the Surface Plasmon Resonance instrument Biacore. Top 3-5 clones will then be expressed and purified to measure the affinity. This method allows selection of humanized antibodies in a full-size IgG format that retain or increase the original affinity of the mouse antibody. Also, in comparison with the above elaborated bacterial phage display based methods, this mammalian cell surface display approach allows selection of high affinity humanized antibodies in a dimeric IgG format selected IgG are immediately good for further downstream applications avoiding time consuming conversion of sc Fv to IgG and codon optimization of converted IgG (for expression in mammalian cells), which sometime deselect some humanized sc Fvs. Also, some good antibodies have sequences that prevent protein synthesis and phage display in bacterial cells these problems can be well overcome in this exclusively mammalian cells based system.

Humanized antibody is defined as a type of antibody made in the laboratory by combining a human antibody with a small part of a mouse or rat monoclonal antibody. The mouse or rat part of the antibody binds to the target antigen, and the human part makes it less likely to be destroyed by the body and immune system. The early success of mouse monoclonal antibodies led to the U.S. Food and Drug. Administration (FDA) approval of the first therapeutic antibody OKT3 (Murom nab) in 1986, as a treatment for kidney transplant rejection. However, most mouse antibodies were shown to have limited use as therapeutic agents because of a short serum half-life, an inability to trigger human effector functions and in particular they were recognized by the patient's immune systems as foreign proteins resulting in human anti-mouse antibodies (HAMA) response. Humanized antibodies are antibodies from non-human species whose protein sequences have been modified to increase their similarity to antibody variants produced naturally in humans. The process of humanization is usually applied to monoclonal antibodies developed for administration to humans (for example, antibodies developed as anti-cancer drugs). Humanization can be necessary when the process of developing a specific antibody involves generation in a non-human immune system. The protein sequences of antibodies produced in this way are partially distinct from homologous antibodies occurring naturally in humans and are therefore potentially immunogenic when administered to human patients. The International Nonproprietary Names of humanized antibodies end in -zumab, as in omalizumab. Humanized antibodies are distinct from chimeric antibodies. The latter also have their protein sequences made more similar to human antibodies, but carry a larger stretch of non-human protein. Humanization is important for reducing the immunogenicity of monoclonal antibodies derived from xenogeneic sources (commonly rodents) and for improving their activation of the human immune system. Since the development of the hybridoma technology, a large number of rodent monoclonal antibodies with specificity for antigens of therapeutic interest have been generated and characterized. Rodent antibodies are highly immunogenic in humans, which limits their clinical applications, especially when repeated administration is required. Importantly, they are rapidly removed from circulation and can cause systemic inflammatory effects as well. As a means of circumventing these problems, we have developed three antibody humanization strategies that can preserve the specificity and affinity of the antibody toward the antigen while significantly or completely eliminating the immunogenicity of the antibody in humans. The first approach is CDR grafting and the second is chain shuffling. These two methods are all based on phage display of humanized sc Fv variants and selection of high-affinity humanized binders through bio-panning. The third method of humanized IgG library screening, is somehow unique where a library of humanized whole IgG to be displayed is made on the surface of mammalian cells and then high-affinity binders will be sorted by FACS.

CDR Grafting & SDR Grafting: A CDR (complementarity-determining region) grafting platform, which is featured with randomization of a small set of framework residues using phage display technology and computer modelling. In this platform, six CDR loops comprising the antigen-binding site are grafted into corresponding human framework regions. Unfortunately, simple grafting of the rodent CDRs into human frameworks does not always reconstitute the binding affinity and specificity of the original antibody because framework residues are involved in antigen binding, either indirectly, by supporting the conformation of the CDR loops, or directly, by contacting the antigen. For this reason, we have developed a computer modeling method to randomize certain framework residues in addition to CDR grafting. The grafted CDRs together with the randomized residues are cloned into a phage display library and the humanized antibodies with the best affinity are selected by screening of the library. This approach allows the epitope specificity of the original antibody to be retained. Of note, humanization by this approach is not 100% since the CDR regions are still of a rodent origin.

To reduce the immunogenicity of CDR-grafted humanized antibodies, the murine content in the CDR-grafted humanized antibodies is minimized through SDR grafting. Within each CDR, there are more variable positions that are directly involved in the interaction with antigen, i.e., specificity-determining residues (SDRs), whereas there are more conserved residues that maintain the conformations of CDRs loops. SDRs may be identified from the 3D structure of the antigen antibody complex and/or the mutational analysis of the CDRs. An SDR-grafted humanized antibody is constructed by grafting the SDRs and the residues maintaining the conformations of the CDRs onto human template, and its immunogenic potential is evaluated by measuring the reactivity to the sera from patients who had been immunized with the parental antibody.

Chain Shuffling: A chain shuffling strategy that is an entirely selective humanization strategy based on the construction and screening of two chimeric phage display libraries. In this approach, the light chain of the rodent antibody is first replaced by light chains in one of our well-tested human antibody libraries the resulting hybrid antibody library is then screened by panning against the particular antigen. After that, the heavy chain of the selected hybrid antibodies is replaced by the heavy chains of the human antibody library. Subsequent screening of this secondary chimeric library will produce fully humanized antibodies. Since phage display library screening mimics in vivo antibody selection and evolution procedure, chain shuffling can result in humanized antibodies whose affinities are higher than that of the original antibody.

Also, this sequential chain shuffling procedure can generate several versions of humanized antibodies with different sequences. The production of multiple humanized antibodies retaining the same epitope specificity is important in therapeutic regimens that call for long-term treatment with antibodies in which anti-idiotypic responses might be avoided by the administration of alternative antibodies. As elaborated above, the chain shuffling method based on chimeric phage display library construction and screening allows full, i.e.

100% humanization of a mouse antibody. A HuScL-2 TM Phage Display Naive Human sc Fv Library with a complexity of 1.42×10 9 transforments as the backbone the chimeric libraries and the donor of human V L and V H chains is proposed (Fig. 9.1).

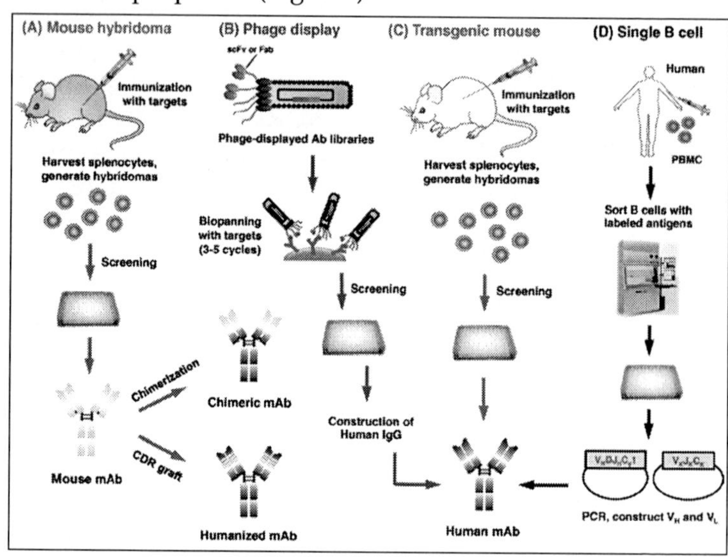

Fig. 9.1 Production of Humanized Antibody

ANTIBODY ENGINEERING USING GENETIC MANIPULATION

Antibodies are proteins secreted by B plasma cells of the immune system to bind antigens and they trigger the immune effector activity. Genetic engineering antibodies are novel recombinant antibodies with improved antigen specificities and effector functions, which are produced by the recombinant DNA and protein engineering technologies. The ability to produce antibodies that are directed against specific antigens drives scientific discovery and the development of clinical diagnosis and therapy.

Types of Antibodies: Antibodies were first discovered at the end of 19th century. In the long process of antibody research, three generations of antibody technology have been developed successively. Firstly, Polyclonal antibodies (pAbs) which are made by different B cell lineages within the higher vertebrates, secondly, monoclonal antibodies (mAbs) which are secreted by a single cell lineage. Kohler and Mlstein first established hybridoma cells by cell hybridization in vitro and acquired a high purity monoclonal antibody for a specific antigen in 1975. By culturing the hybridoma cells in vitro, a large number of monoclonal antibodies are obtained and these antibodies are highly specificity because of which they are widely used in cell biology, basic medicine, clinical diagnosis and other fields. Thirdly, are the antibodies which are genetically engineered antibodies, and are made by the application of modern recombinant DNA or gene mutation technology to reconstruct gene fragments and obtain specific antibodies through cell transfection and culture in vitro.

Engineered Antibody: Antibody engineering consists of modifying monoclonal antibody (mAb) sequences and/ or structures to either enhance or dampen their functions. Monoclonal Abs have revolutionized the fields of diagnosis and immunotherapy for the treatment of a variety of diseases, particularly in cancer therapy. A challenging issue remains the production of therapeutic m Abs and Ab-derived drugs with the highest objective response rate in patients and the lowest toxicity. Therefore, Ab engineering is a major translational research topic which aims at producing highly specific and effective mAbs, with optimal processing, stability, and tolerance. Therefore, Ab engineering is a major translation which aims at producing highly specific and effective m Abs, with optimal processing, stability, and tolerance.

Features of Genetically Engineered Antibody- Genetically engineered antibody consist of following features:

- The variable region specifically binds one antigen
- The "fragment crystallizable" Fc in the constant region mediates effector functions, such as antibody-dependent cellular cytotoxicity (ADCC), antibody-dependent cellular phagocytosis (ADCP), or complement-dependent cytotoxicity (CDC).

- Design, generate and purify your mAbs
- Assess and compare the functions of your mAbs using our cellular assays and our extensive clinically-relevant mAb collection.

Antibody Generation: Production of recombinant monoclonal antibodies (mAbs) is important in the studying and developing novel antibody-based treatments for a number of diseases including cancer. Antibody production requires DNA technology to express the mAb of interest, mammalian cells for their production, because of their high-yielding expression in both as transient and stable cell lines and affinity chromatography to purify the final mAb. Optimization of the expression vector before transfection into mammalian cells is indispensable in ensuring that the mAb production is sufficient and accurate. There are many plasmids to meet your mAb-producing needs and the plasmid backbones have been optimized to ensure ideal expression under the control of composite promoters. In addition, our plasmids contain unique multiple cloning sites (MCSs) for the insertion of variable regions of any given MAb. Whether one wants to change the effector function of one's MAb or just wants to maximize one's MAb production (Fig. 9.2), there are two families of MAb-producing plasmids which include:

- **pFUSE:** An exhaustive collection of plasmids designed to change a mAb from one isotype to another enabling the generation of MAbs with the same antigen affinity but different effector functions.
- **pTRIOZ:** A collection of plasmids designed for high-yield whole mAb production using a single plasmid.

Antibody Purification: For fast and efficient purification of IgA antibodies from biological samples, Peptide M also provides Protein G for IgG purification, and Protein L for purification of both IgG and IgA. The correct choice of purification method depends upon the immunoglobulin class, the species in which it was raised and the intended use of the antibodies. Antibodies from tissue culture supernatant, serum or ascites can be purified using one or more of the following antibody binding proteins.

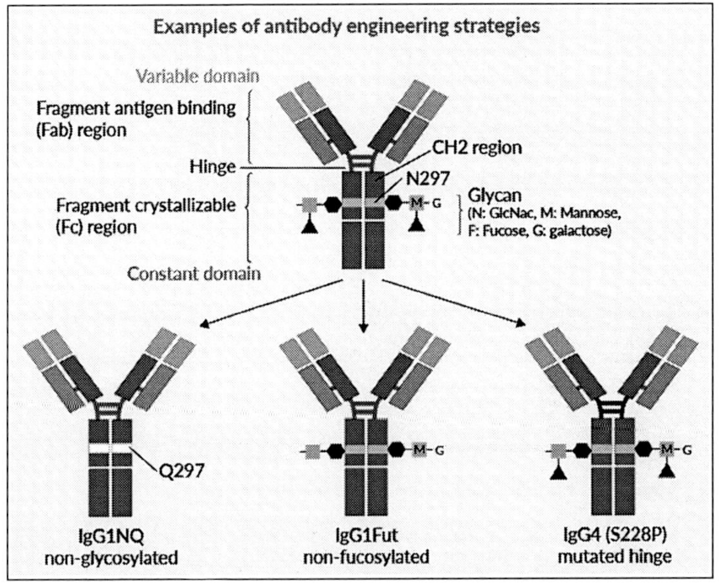

Fig. 9.2: Genetically Engineered Antibodies

Applications of Genetically Engineered Antibody: Engineered antibodies have varied applications which include:

1. Antibody engineering plays a major role in the prevention of cancer disease.
2. The development of different types of antibodies is the central approach for the treatment of various diseases and eliminating the infection.
3. Polyclonal antibodies are different concentrations among antibodies and they are not used clinically often.
4. Antibody engineering for Polyclonal antibodies are not so popular and working for the treatments prospectus.
5. Engineered monoclonal antibodies are under the examination and research phase and require deep study for the treatment of severe diseases.

6. Monoclonal Antibodies further focuses on the development of antibody engineering with a view that it can help in the treatment of autoimmune systems.
7. The large revenue of the antibody services is pushing the biotechnological companies in manufacturing the engineered antibodies by clinical tests and experiments. This can be expected to see a drastic change shortly due to increased demands and increased interest in biotechnological companies.

RECOMBINANT PROTEIN

Recombinant protein is a manipulated form of protein, which is generated in various ways to produce large quantities of proteins with modified gene sequences. The formation of recombinant protein is carried out in specialized vehicles known as vectors and manufactured useful commercial products. Recombinant Protein is a protein encoded by a gene recombinant DNA that has been cloned in a system which supports expression of the gene and translation of messenger RNA. Modification of the gene by recombinant DNA technology can lead to expression of a mutant protein. Recombinant protein is generally produced by application of recombinant DNA technology in which a desired gene is inserted in a vector.

Production of Recombinant Protein: It is typically achieved by the manipulation of gene expression in an organism such that it expresses large amounts of a recombinant gene. In order to get enough amount of the protein of interest, strain selection, codon optimization, fusion systems, co-expression, mutagenesis and isotope labeling techniques are usually used. For, the production of a recombinant protein primarily the gene of interest is isolated and is then inserted into a proper vector i.e., Plasmid, Cosmid or Phage. The production of protein requires following steps to be followed in sequential manner.

Amplification of gene of interest: The separation process may separate the protein and non-protein parts of the mixture, and finally separate the desired protein from all other proteins. The purification scheme of a protein must be optimized to complete this process firstly, selecting the right lysis reagents and appropriate purification resin. Most recombinant proteins are expressed as fusion proteins with short affinity tags, such as poly histidine or glutathione S-transferase, which allow for selective purification of the protein of interest.

Insert into cloning vector: The desired gene is inserted into cloning vector which may be cosmid, plasmid or phage. The vector is a vehicle where the gene can replicate and multiply itself to produce its copies, while selecting a vector it should be kept in mind that the vector should have the capacity to multiply gene to its maximum.

Sub cloning into expression vector: The gene containing vector is then screened and the vectors and the vectors which contains gene are then inserted into a proper host where the gene can multiply and produce its copies.

Transformation into protein expressing host: The vector is then inserted into a proper host where the gene can make its copies and can undergo transcription and translation to form desired protein. The host can be bacteria (*E. coli*), yeast, mammalian cells or Baculovirus-insect cell system.

Test for identification of recombinant protein: The next step is the identification of desired protein, which checks that whether the desired protein has been produced in body of the host or not this is usually done by use of Western blot or Fluorescence technique.

Large scale production: If the desired protein to be produced is in large quantity then it is done in a fermenter preferably a large scale fermenter, where the host generally *E.coli* or Yeast is provided with media and optimum growth conditions in which the cells are destined to make protein.

Isolation and purification: The final step is the identification of the recombinant protein which involves a number of processes, including pumping. ultrafiltration, and significant shear environments. More importantly, protein tags are useful and convenient tool for improving solubility of recombinant proteins, streaming protein purification, and allowing an easy way to track proteins during protein expression and purification (Fig. 9.3).

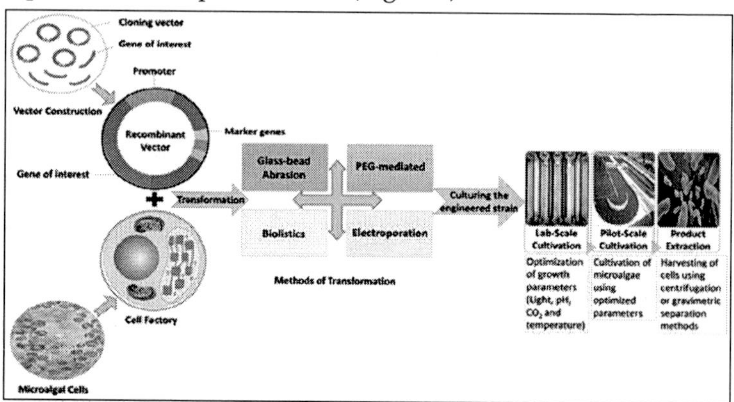

Fig. 9.3. Production of Recombinant Protein

Types of Recombinant Protein: Basically, therapeutic proteins can be classified into four groups:

Group I: This group includes therapeutic proteins with enzymatic or regulatory activity and are capable of replacing a protein that is deficient or abnormal, up-regulate an existing pathway, or provide a new function or activity.

Group II: This group of therapeutic proteins includes proteins with special targeting activity and these proteins interfere with a molecule or organism or deliver other molecules.

Group III: This category of therapeutic proteins include proteins which behave as vaccines, these proteins help protect against foreign agents, autoimmune diseases, and cancer.

Group IV: This group of therapeutic protein includes proteins which can be used for diagnostic purpose. These proteins are generally purified and recombinant proteins.

Applications of Recombinant Protein- Recombinant Protein has following applications:

1. **Medicine:** Recombinant proteins provide important therapies for a variety of diseases, such as diabetes, cancer, infectious diseases, hemophilia, and anemia. Common therapeutic proteins include antibodies, FC fusion proteins, hormones, interleukins, enzymes, and anticoagulants. There is a growing demand for recombinant proteins of therapeutic applications. Currently, most of all recombinant therapeutic proteins are produced in mammalian cells because these cells are capable of producing high-quality proteins similar to the naturally occurring ones. In addition, many approved recombinant therapeutic proteins are generated in *E.coli* due to its well-characterized genetics, rapid growth, and high-yield production.
2. **Recombinant Proteins:** They help to elucidate the basic and fundamental principles of an organism. These molecules can be used to identify and locate the position of the protein encoded by a specific gene, and to uncover the function of other genes in various cellular activities such as cell signaling, metabolism, growth, replication and death, transcription, translation, and protein modification. Thus, recombinant proteins are frequently used in molecular biology, cell biology, biochemistry, structural and biophysical studies, and many other research fields.
3. **Understanding protein-protein interaction:** Recombinant proteins are useful tools in understanding protein-protein interactions. They have proved their performance in several laboratory techniques, such as ELISA, Western Blot and immunohistochemistry (IHC). Recombinant proteins can be used to develop enzymatic assays, when used in conjunction with a matched antibody pair, recombinant proteins can be used as standards such as ELISA standards. Moreover, recombinant proteins can be used as positive controls in Western blots.

4. **Biotechnology:** Recombinant proteins are also used in industry, food production, agriculture, and bioengineering. For example, in breeding industry, enzymes can be added to animal feed to increase the nutritional value of feed ingredients, reduce feed and waste management costs, support animal gut health, enhance animal performance and improve the environment. Besides, lactic acid bacteria (LAB) have been used from a long time for the production of fermented foods, and recently, LAB has been engineered for the expression of recombinant proteins, which would have wide applications such as improving human/ animal digestion and nutrition.
5. **Recombinant Protein and Diseases:** Recombinant Proteins are widely used for curing diseases. Alpha-1-antitrypsin is a protein made by the liver, is secreted to the bloodstream, and then circulates the body to protect the lung. The patients who can not produce the protein usually regularly and quantitatively receive an infusion of Alpha-1-antitrypsin protein, which is extracted from donor blood. Researchers also improve the proteins by genetic techniques, there by obtaining recombinant therapeutic proteins similar to human versions with a specific sugar-structure, it is likely to eliminate the need for human donors in the future.
6. **Recombinant Protein and Vaccines:** Human papillomavirus, referred to as HPV, not only causes cervical cancer in women, certain strains but also have been linked to head and neck cancers in men. Currently, Gardasil-9 vaccine is used to prevent the virus. Gardasil 9 is nine of these individual vaccines mixed into one, which can protect against multiple variants of HPV but, it is relatively expensive so that few people can afford it

Limitations of Recombinant Proteins: However, recombinant proteins also have limitations which include following:

1. In some cases, the production of recombinant proteins is complex, expensive, and time-consuming.
2. The recombinant proteins produced in cells may not be the same as the natural forms. This difference may reduce the effectiveness of therapeutic recombinant proteins and even cause side effects, additionally, this difference may affect the results of experiments.
3. A major concern for all recombinant drugs is immunogenicity. All biotechnologically produced therapeutics may exhibit some form of immunogenicity so, It is difficult to predict the safety of novel therapeutic proteins.

SOUTHERN BLOTTING

Southern blotting is the process of transfer of DNA fragments that are separated by electrophoresis onto a membrane for immobilization and identification. This technique has been adopted as a routine procedure for the analysis of DNA samples for different applications. It was discovered by Edwin Southern, and the technique has been named after him. The technique formed the basis of other important techniques like Western Blotting and Northern Blotting that are based on the same principle. The technique is basically used to determine the size of a DNA fragment from a complex mixture of genomic DNA. The technique is also relatively quantitative and can be used to determine the number of copies of a segment present in a genome. On, the basis of membrane choice, transfer buffer and method the technique can be modified to some extend. Most commonly used membrane includes nitrocellulose membrane because of its robust nature and the capability of being re-probed a number of times. Southern Blotting utilizes radioactive probes, whereas other labeling system use fluorescence and chemiluminescence. The technique has been modified in a number of ways to better serve the application and has been made more complex and efficient.

Principle of Southern Blot: The principle of southern blotting is similar to the blotting technique involving the transfer of biomolecules from a membrane to another for detection and identification. The DNA to be analyzed is digested with restriction enzymes and fractionated by size by the process of agarose gel electrophoresis. The DNA strands are denatured by alkaline treatment and are transferred to a nylon or nitrocellulose membrane by the blotting process. The strands on the membrane are immobilized on the surface by baking or UV irradiation. The DNA sequences on the membrane can be detected by the process of hybridization. Hybridization reactions are specific as the probes used bind to target fragments consisting of complementary sequences. The probes used are labeled with different components that can be visualized by different methods depending on the type of probes used.

Requirements: There are mainly three requirements for southern blot viz. equipment, material, solutions and buffer.

Equipment: Water bath, agarose gel, power supply, UV radiation, Hybridization oven, Hybridization bottles, trays, Film processor, Pipettes, Centrifuge tubes, Glass plate, Whatman 3 mm chromatography paper, Nylon membrane/ Nitrocellulose membrane, Syringe, Cellulose acetate membrane.

Material: Restriction Enzymes, Restriction enzymes buffer, Agarose, TBE buffer, DNA loading buffer, Tris base, Sodium chloride, Sodium hydroxide, Sodium citrate, DNA labeling kit, Nucleic acid detection kit, Sodium dodecyl sulfate (SDS), Polyvinyl pyrrolidone, Bovine serum albumin, Formaldehyde and Phenol.

Solutions and Buffers: These include denaturation buffer (NaOH and NaCl in the ratio 1:6), neutralization buffer (Tris-HCl and NaCl in the ratio 5:3), SSC includes 175.3 g of NaCl and 88.2 g of Sodium citrate to 1L of distilled water, detection buffer like tris-HCl and NaCl in the ratio 5:1.

Procedure of Southern Blot: The procedure of Southern Blot is completed in the following manner.

Restriction, Digestion of DNA: About 10 µg of the extracted genomic DNA is digested with the appropriate restriction enzyme in a micro centrifuge tube. The tube is incubated overnight at 37° C. In some cases, the tubes are heated in a water bath at 65° C for 20 minutes after the incubation to denature the restriction enzymes. To the tubes, 10µl of the DNA sample buffer is added, and the mixture is poured on agarose gel for electrophoresis.

Electrophoresis: The percentage and size of the gel are determined based on the size of the DNA fragments to be separated. The gel is then prepared accordingly. The electrophoresis buffer is prepared with ethidium bromide and poured into the tank in a way that is a few millimeters above the gel support. The gel cast is prepared along with a comb with teeth to form wells that can hold the sample volume. Once the comb is in place, the gel is slowly poured into the cast. Once the gel has set, the comb is removed, and the gel is placed on the tank. Running buffer is added to the tank to cover the gel. The samples are prepared by adding loading buffer and carefully pipetted into the wells. The tank is connected to the power supply and allowed to run overnight (Fig. 9.4).

Denaturation: The gel is removed from the electrophoresis apparatus and is placed in a glass tray with 500 ml denaturation buffer (1.5 M NaCl and 0.5 M NaOH) for 45 minutes at room temperature. The denaturation buffer is poured off and replaced with a neutralization buffer. The gel is allowed to soak for 1 hour while slowly rotating on a platform rotator.

Blotting: An oblong sponge that is slightly larger than the gel is placed on a glass dish which is filled with SSC to leave the soaked sponge about half-submerged in the buffer. Three pieces of whatman 3mm paper are cut the same size as the sponge. These are placed on the sponge and wet with

SSC after which the gel is placed on the filter paper and squeezed out to remove bubbles by rolling a glass pipette over the surface. A nylon membrane, just large enough to cover the surface of the gel is placed on top of the gel. The membrane is further flooded with SSC, and few sheets of filter paper are placed on top of it. Finally, a glass plate is laid on top of the structure to hold everything in place, the DNA transfer is allowed to occur overnight.

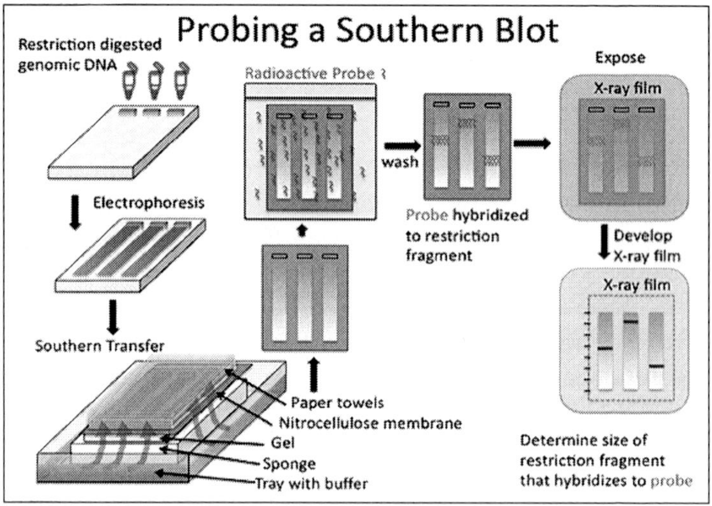

Fig. 9.4: Separation of DNA Fragments

Baking/Immobilization: The nylon membrane is removed from the blotting structure and is attached to a vacuum or regular oven at 80° C for 2-3 hours. The DNA strands on the membrane can also be immobilized by exposing the membrane to ultraviolet radiation.

Hybridization: The membrane is exposed to the hybridization probe, which can either be a DNA fragment or an RNA segment with a specific sequence that detects the target DNA. The probe nucleic acid is labeled so that it can be detected by incorporating radioactivity or tagging the molecules with fluorescent or chromogenic dye. The conditions during the process are chosen in a way that the probe hybridizes the target DNA with a complementary sequence on the membrane. The hybridization is followed by washing with a buffer to remove the probe that is bound nonspecifically or remain unbound so that only labeled probes remain bound to the target sequence.

Detection: The hybridized regions on the membrane can be detected via autoradiography by placing the nylon membrane in contact with a photographic film. The images indicate the position of the hybridized DNA molecules, which can be used to determine the length of the fragments by comparing them with the marker DNA molecules of known length. Similarly, the images also provide information about the number of the hybridizing fragments and their size. If a fluorescent or a chromogenic dye is used, these can be visualized on X-ray film or by the development of color on the membrane.

Result and Interpretation of Southern Blot: The results of a Southern blot are observed in the form of bands on the membrane. The size of the DNA fragments can be determined by comparing their relative size with the DNA bands of known lengths.

Applications of Southern Blot: The applications of Southern Blot include following-

1. Southern blotting has many applications in the field of gene discovery, mapping, evolution, and diagnostic studies.
2. The technique can be used for DNA analysis to detect point mutations and other structural rearrangements in the DNA sequences.
3. The method also allows the determination of molecular weights of the restriction fragments, which helps in the analysis of such fragments.
4. Since the technique enables the detection of a particular DNA segment, it can be used in personal identification via fingerprinting.
5. It can be used in disease diagnosis as well as prenatal diagnosis of genetic diseases.

Limitations of Southern Blot: The limitations of Southern Blot include following-

1. The method is costly as it requires expensive equipment and reagents as compared to other tests.
2. It is a complex process consisting of multiple steps. The process is also labour intensive that requires trained personnel.
3. It is a time-consuming process that can be replaced by other faster processes like Polymerase Chain Reaction.
4. It is a semi-quantitative process that only provides estimated sizing of the DNA fragments.
5. Southern blotting is not a suitable method for detecting mutations at the base-pair level.
6. The sample requires a large amount of sample and higher quality of DNA via superior isolation methods.

NORTHERN BLOT

Northern Blot may be defined as a technique which is based on the principle of blotting for the analysis of specific RNA in a complex mixture. The technique was discovered after Southern Blotting and is a modified version of the Southern Blotting used for the analysis of DNA sequences. The detection of certain sequences of nucleic acids extracted from different types of biological samples is essential in molecular biology, which makes blotting techniques imperative in the field. The principle is identical to southern blotting except for the probes used for the detection as northern blotting detects RNA sequences. This technique provides information about the length of the RNA sequences and the presence of variations in the sequence. Even though the technique is primarily focused on the identification of RNA sequences, it has also been used for the quantification of RNA sequences. Since the discovery of the technique, several modifications have been made in the technique for the analysis of mRNAs, pre-mRNAs, and short RNAs. Northern blotting was employed as the primary technique for the analysis of RNA fragments for a long time however, new, more convenient and cost-effective techniques like RT-PCR have slowly replaced the technique.

Principle of Northern Blotting: The principle of the northern blot is the same as all other blotting technique that is based on the transfer of biomolecules from one membrane to another.

- The RNA samples are separated on gels according to their size by gel electrophoresis. Since RNAs are single-stranded, these can form secondary structures by intermolecular base pairing. The electrophoretic separation of the RNA segments is thus performed under denaturing conditions.
- The separated RNA fragments are then transferred to a nylon membrane. Nitrocellulose membrane is not used as RNA doesn't bind effectively to the membrane.
- The transferred segments are immobilized onto the membrane by fixing agents. The RNA fragments on the membrane are detected by the addition of a labeled probe complementary to the RNA sequences present on the membrane.
- The hybridization forms the basis of the detection of RNA as the specificity of hybridization between the probe, and the RNA allows the accurate identification of the segments.
- Northern blot utilizes size-dependent separation of RNA segments and thus can be used to determine the sizes of the transcripts.

Equipment: Agarose gel cast, power supply, microwave, centrifuge, heating block, UV cross linker, hybridization oven, hybridization vessels, vials, forceps, pipettes, glass tubes.

Material: Agarose gel, Sodium citrate, Ethylenediaminetetraacetic acid disodium salt dehydrate, NaOH, HCl, Formaldehyde, Glycerol, Ethidium bromide, Bromophenol Blue, RNA ladder, $MgCl_2$, NaCl, Polyvinyl pyrrolidone,

Bovine Serum Albumin, SDS, NaH_2PO_4, Tris-HCl, Triton-X, DTT, Taq buffer, Taq polymerase.

Procedure of Northern Blot: Northern Blotting is accomplished in following steps-

Separation of RNA Fragments: The RNA gel solution is prepared by adding formaldehyde to the agarose solution. The cast is assembled, and the prepared denaturing gel is poured into the cast.

As the gel begins to set, a comb with appropriate teeth is added to form wells. Once the gel is set, the comb is removed, and the gel is equilibrated with a running buffer for 30 minutes before running and µg RNA sample is mixed with an equal volume of RNA loading buffer. Three µg of RNA markers are added in the same volume of RNA loading buffer. The samples are incubated at 65°C on a heating block for about 12-15 minutes. The samples are loaded to the equilibrated gel, and the first row of wells is filled with RNA markers, the gel is then run at 125V for about 3 hours (Fig. 9.5).

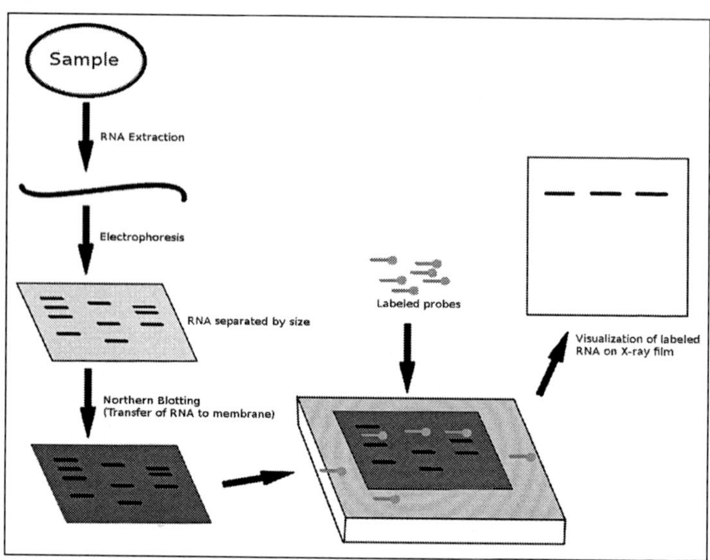

Fig. 9.5: Process of Northern Blotting

Transfer of RNA from gel to nylon membrane: A nylon membrane is cut that is larger than the size of the denaturing gel, and a filter paper with the same size as the nylon membrane is also prepared. Once the electrophoresis process is complete, the RNA gel is removed from the tank and rinsed with water. An oblong sponge that is slightly larger than the gel is placed on a glass dish, and the dish is filled with SSC to a point so as to leave the soaked sponge about half-submerged in the buffer. A few pieces of Whatman 3mm papers are placed on top of the sponge and are wetted with SSC buffer. The gel is then placed on top of the filter paper and squeezed out to remove air bubbles by rolling a glass pipette over the surface. The nylon membrane prepared is wetted with distilled water on an RNase-free dish for about 5 minutes. The wetted membrane is placed on the surface of the gel while avoiding any air bubbles formation. The surface is further flooded with SSC, and a few more filter papers are placed on top of the membrane. A glass plate is placed on top of the structure in order to hold everything in place and the structure is left overnight to obtain an effective transfer.

Immobilization: Once the transfer is complete, the gel is removed and rinsed with SSC, and allowed to dry. The membrane is placed between two pieces of filter paper and baked in a vacuum oven at 80° C for 2 hours. In some cases, the membrane can be wrapped in a UV transparent plastic wrap and irradiates for an appropriate time on a UV trans illuminator.

Hybridization: The RNA probes to be used are to be labeled to a specific activity of >108 d pm/µg, and unincorporated nucleotides are to be removed. The membrane carrying the immobilized RNA is wetted with SSC and the membrane is placed in a hybridization tube with the RNA-side-up, and 1 ml of formaldehyde solution is added. The tube is placed in the hybridization oven and incubated at 42° C for 3 hours. If the probe used is double-stranded, it is denatured by heating in a water bath or incubator for 10 minutes at 100° C. The desired volume of the probe is pipette into the hybridization tube and further incubated at 42° C. The solution is poured off, and the membrane is washed with a wash solution, the membrane is then observed under autoradiography.

Result and Interpretation of Northern Blot: The RNA bands are observed under radiography in the form of bands. The distance of the bands from the markers can be used to determine the length and semi quantification of the RNA fragments.

Applications of Northern Blotting: The applications of Northern Blotting include following-

1. The technique can be used for the identification and separation of RNA fragments collected from different biological sources.
2. Northern blotting is used as a sensitive test for the detection of transcription of DNA fragments that are to be used as a probe in Southern Blotting.
3. It also allows the detection and quantification of specific mRNAs from different tissues and different living organisms.
4. Northern blotting is used as a tool for gene expression studies related to overexpression of cancer-causing genes, and gene expression during transplant rejects.
5. Northern blotting has been used as a molecular tool for the diagnosis of diseases like Crohn's disease.
6. The process is used as a method for the detection of viral microRNAs that play important roles in viral infection.

WESTERN BLOT

Western Blot, also known as immunoblotting, is the process of separating proteins and identifying them in a complex biological sample. The process requires use of polyacrylamide in order to separate proteins prior to their identification. In this process the proteins which are separated by SDS-PAGE and are absorbed onto absorbent membrane which are then identified on the membrane by different means. The technique uses antibody probes against membrane bound proteins and finds wide applications in biochemistry and other sciences as it can detect and characterize a multitude of proteins. The sensitivity of the process depends on the efficiency of transfer retention of proteins during processing and the final detection. Western blotting or protein blotting depends on the specificity of interaction between the protein of interest and the probe used for the detection of the protein. Unlike Southern blotting that utilizes radio-labeled nucleic acid probes, western blotting usually uses a second antibody tagged with an enzyme. Western blotting has a number of advantages over other similar techniques as the process only requires the use of a small amount of reagents, and the same protein transfer can be used for multiple analyses.

Principle of Western Blotting: The principle of western blotting is the interaction between the proteins and the probes used for the detection of the proteins. The proteins used for western blotting are separated by gel electrophoresis to obtain them on a gel matrix. The proteins are then transferred to a nitrocellulose or poly vinylidene fluoride (PVDF) membrane, where they are immobilized and the transfer of the protein is known as blotting. The protein on the membrane can either be detected by the use of a reporter-labeled primary antibody directed against the protein or a reporter-labeled secondary antibody directed at the primary antibody. The reporter or probe present on the antibody can be an enzyme that produces a color reaction or a luminescent signal at the antigen-antibody binding site that produces a fluorescent signal in the presence of a particular substrate. The signal or color generated by the probe requires a detection system that is appropriate for the signal or intensity generated.

Requirements of Western Blotting: Gel (Nu PAGE), Basic Power Supply, Sample buffer, Heating block, Sample reducing buffer, Pre-stained protein ladder, Mini Trans-Blot consisting of a tank, lid, and a blot module. The assembly is stored with cooling ice so that it is frozen when needed, 0.45 µm nitrocellulose filter paper, PAGE transfer buffer, Methanol, Square Pyrex dish, Square disposable plastic Petri dish, Razorblade and gel knife, Basic power supply, 10x Tris-buffered saline with 1% between 20, Shaker, 10% powdered nonfat dry milk, Square disposable plastic Petri dish, Plastic pouches, Impulse heat sealer, Primary antibody, Secondary antibody conjugated with horseradish peroxidase against the host species of the primary antibody. Chemiluminescent substrate, Gel documentation system

Procedure of Western Blot: The process of western blotting consists of the following steps-

Sample Preparation: The most commonly used samples for western blot are cell lysates which are collected by the process of extraction. The extraction can be achieved by different means like mechanical destruction, chemical extraction, or the use of enzymes. The extraction of often performed at cold temperature in the presence of protease inhibitors in order to prevent the denaturation of the proteins.

Gel Electrophoresis: The protein sample is diluted with the sample buffer, is heated and shaken for 10 minutes at 70° C after this, the sample is then centrifuged at 5000g. The gel case is removed from the pouch and is placed in the buffer tank against the rubber seal with the gel walls facing inside of the tank reservoir. The running buffer is poured onto the upper reservoir while ensuring that no buffer leakage occurs on the lower tank. Each of the wells is then loaded with an equal volume of heat-denatured sample, and one of the lanes is reserved for the protein ladder. The lid is placed on the tank, and it is connected to the power supply and the run is allowed to run at 200 V constant for 50 minutes.

Protein Transfer: The transfer buffer is prepared by adding 10% methanol to the buffer. The transfer case is taken and laid out and is then covered with a transfer buffer. A foam sponge is taken and laid on the backside, over which goes the filter paper which are placed to ensure that both of them are wet and slightly submerged. The gel is taken out from the tank and placed on the wet filter paper and the nitrocellulose membrane is wet with the transfer buffer and is placed on top of the gel in a way that there are no bubbles between the gel and the membrane. The transfer case is placed into the transfer tank, which is further filled with transfer buffer after which, the tank is connected to power at 100V for 1 hour. Once, the transfer is complete, the transfer case is removed, and the nitrocellulose membrane is removed from the gel.

Immunodetection: The membrane is washed with tris-buffered saline for 5 minutes in a Petri dish. The 10% nonfat dry milk is mixed with the tris buffer, and the membrane is covered with the mixture for 30 minutes at room temperature. The membrane is washed with the tris buffer to remove any excess mixture remaining on the membrane. With the help of the forceps, the membrane is transferred to a new Petri dish onto which the primary antibody is added. The membrane with the antibody is incubated for 3 hours at room temperature. The membrane is washed after incubation with the tris buffer. The membrane is transferred again to a new Petri dish, where a secondary HRP-conjugated antibody is added. The membrane is incubated for 1 hour. The concentration of secondary antibodies often remains at 1 μg/ml, but this also depends on the dilution. The membrane is washed again with Tris buffer to remove excess antibodies from the surface (Fig. 9.6). The membrane is incubated with the substrate for 5 minutes, and the observation is made.

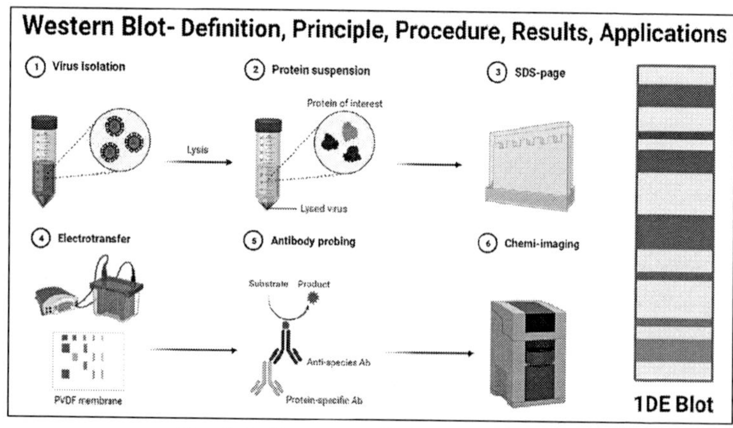

Fig. 9.6: Process of Western Blotting

Result and Interpretation of Western Blot: The result of western blotting depends on the type of probes used during the process. If an enzyme-conjugated secondary antibody is used, the reaction between the substrate and the enzyme produces a color. The soluble dye is converted into an insoluble form, resulting in a different color on the membrane. In order to stop the development of a blot, the dye is removed by washing the membrane and the protein levels can then be evaluated by spectrophotometry.

Applications of Western Blotting- There are many different applications of Western Blotting which include:

1. Western blotting is an excellent method with high sensitivity in order to detect a particular protein even in low quantity.
2. Western blotting has been used in the clinical diagnosis of different diseases. The confirmatory test for HIV involves a western blot by detecting anti-HIV antibodies in the serum.
3. The technique has been used to quantify proteins and other gene products in gene expression studies.
4. Since western blotting detects the proteins by their size and ability to bind to the antibody, it is appropriate

for evaluating the protein expressions in cells and further analysis of protein fractions during protein purification.

5. Western blotting is also used for the analysis of different biomarkers like growth factors, cytokines, and hormones.

IMMUNO PCR

PCR is a technique which is used to amplify a specific segment of DNA, and can be performed using only a very small amount of starting material. It employs a three-step cycling process in which the first step is heat-induced denaturation of dsDNA to separate the two complementary strands, secondly the temperature is reduced to allow binding of PCR primers and thirdly, the use of DNA polymerase to produce a complimentary copy of the target DNA sequence. During traditional PCR, the amplified DNA is run on a gel and stained with ethidium bromide. The immuno-PCR method is developed in the year, 1992 by *T Sano, L Smith and R Cantor and in this method a* primary antibody is immobilized on the surface of the plate which binds with the conjugates that facilitate immunoreaction as well as the amplification reaction. The "Conjugate" mentioned here, is the secondary antibody that is bound/ conjugated with the oligonucleotide primer used in the PCR reaction (Fig. 9.7). The antibody-bound oligonucleotides amplify the DNA and are detected.

Process of PCR: The steps of the immuno-PCR/ IPCR are described in the figure below and *the actual process of immuno-PCR involves following steps-*

- In the first step, the primary antibodies are immobilized to the surface of the reaction tube, similar to that in case of ELISA.
- In the next step, the sample molecules are bound to the primary antibody and they make the conjugate.
- The unbounded sample molecules are washed off by the washing buffer.

- After that, the oligonucleotide linked or the primer-linked secondary antibody is added to the tube.
- In the next step, it immediately reacts with the secondary antibody-oligonucleotide-linked conjugate.
- The excess conjugates are removed by washing.
- Now our sample is ready for amplification.
- In each cycle, the primer bind with the template DNA and amplify it, the amplification is detected by the machine and recorded.
- The amplicons are determined and so is the antigen which is conjugated with it.
- Ultimately, the sample is quantitatively determined.

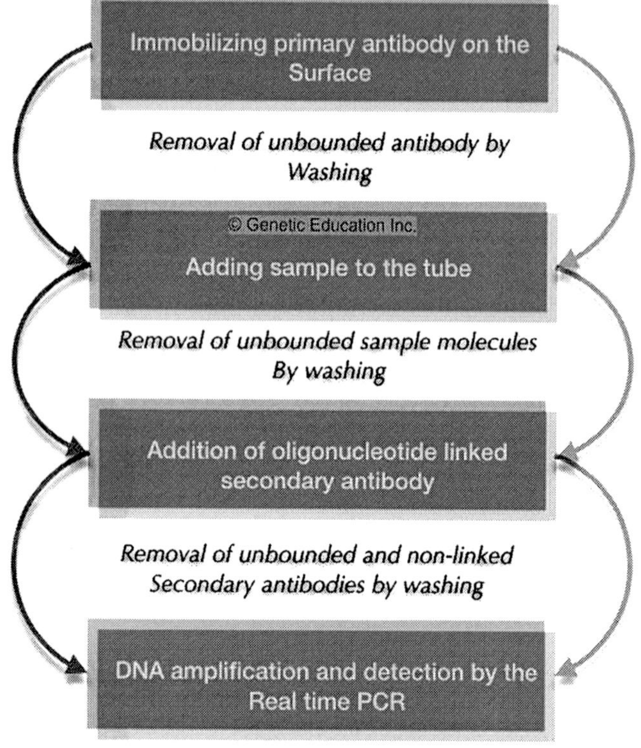

Fig. 9.7: Steps of Immuno PCR

Merits of Immuno PCR: There are some applications of immune PCR which include-

- The immuno-PCR facilitates the detection of an extremely low level of antigen which is not possible in the traditional ELISA.
- We can even detect a pictogram of the concentration of particular analytes present in the sample.
- The method is rapid and time-efficient a lot of incubation steps are required in the ELISA, which are not needed in the immuno-PCR. Hence it is fast, accurate and rapid.
- The reproducibility is very high and the detection range is wider than the ELISA method.
- Further, one can detect multiple samples at once.

Limitations of Immuno PCR: Despite of so many advantages immune PCR has some limitations which include-

- Conjugating oligonucleotides with the antibody required time and expertise.
- The conjugation process is time-consuming, tedious and hard. Also, the cost of preparing a conjugate is very high.
- Albeit, the IPCR technique has power and potential, advancement and automation are not available easily.
- The specificity and sensitivity of the IPCR or qiPCR are 1000-fold higher than the ELISA method.
- Furthermore, fewer research data are available on the IPCR.
- The success rate of conjugate preparation is very low and a large portion of the oligonucleotide primers are washed off during the washing.
- This is the reason why it is time-consuming and costly and because of that scientists are not interested in the automation of immuno-PCR.

POINTS TO REMEMBER

1. Immunobiotechnology refers to combination of immunology and biotechnology which aids in finding new methods of disease diagnosis and cure thus helping in the identification of novel therapeutic targets.
2. Common immunobiotechnological techniques include production of humanized antibodies, antibody engineering using genetic manipulation, recombinant protein, Southern Blotting, Northern Blotting, Western Blotting and Immuno-PCR.
3. Humanized antibody refers to a combined antibody which is synthesized by combining human gene with gene of other species.
4. Recombinant Proteins are the proteins which are synthesized by inserting a desired gene into a vector and vector is inserted into a proper host where the synthesis of proteins takes place.
5. Southern Blotting refers to the technique used for identifying the unknown DNA sequences.
6. Northern Blotting refers to the technique used for identifying the unknown RNA sequences.
7. Immuno PCR is a method in which a primary antibody is immobilized on the surface of the plate which binds with the conjugates that facilitate immunoreaction as well as the amplification reaction.

QUESTIONS

1. Explain in detail about important immunotechniques?
2. Write a short note on recombinant proteins?
3. Explain in brief about production of humanized antibodies?
4. Explain in brief about antibody engineering using genetic manipulation?
5. Explain in detail about Northern Blotting?
6. Explain in detail about Western Blotting?
7. Explain in detail about Southern Blotting?

Laboratory Experiments

DETERMINATION OF BLOOD GROUP

Experiment 1st: Determination of blood group.

Aim: The main purpose of conducting this experiment is to understand the basic concept of the ABO blood group system and to know our blood group and type.

Theory: During the blood transfusion, the two most important group systems examined are the *ABO-system* and the *Rhesus system.*

ABO-system: The basis of ABO grouping is of two antigens- Antigen A and Antigen B. The ABO grouping system is classified into four types based on the presence or absence of antigens on the red blood cells surface and plasma antibodies.

- **Group A** – contains antigen A and antibody B.
- **Group B** – contains antigen B and antibody A.
- **Group AB** – contains both A and B antigen and no antibodies (neither A nor B).
- **Group O** – contains neither A nor B antigen and both antibodies A and B.

The ABO group system is important during blood donation or blood transfusion as mismatching of blood group can lead to clumping of red blood cells with various disorders. It is important for the blood cells to match while transfusing i.e. donor-recipient compatibility is necessary. For example, a person of blood group A can receive blood either from group A or O as there are no antibodies for A and O in blood group A.

(a) **Rh Blood group system:** In addition to the ABO blood grouping system, the other prominent one is the Rh blood group system. About two-thirds of the population contains the third antigen on the surface of their red blood cells known as *Rh factor* or *Rh antigen*; this decides whether the blood group is positive or negative. If the Rh factor is present, an individual is *rhesus positive* (Rh+ve); if an Rh factor is absent individual is *rhesus negative* (Rh-ve) as they produce Rh antibodies. Therefore, compatibility between donor and individual is crucial in this case as well.

Requirements: Sterilized needles, Blood sample, alcohol swabs, clean slide, sterile cotton balls, anti-A, B and D and all these equipment are available in the kit.

Procedure:

- Take a clean glass slide and draw three circles on it.
- Unpack the Monoclonal Antibodies (MAB) kit. In the first circle add Anti-A, to the second circle add Anti-B and to the third circle add Anti-D with the help of a dropper.
- Keep the slide aside safely without disturbing.
- Now wipe the ring finger with the alcohol swabs and rub gently near the fingertip, where the blood sample will be collected.
- Prick the ring fingertip with the lancet and wipe off the first drop of the blood.

- As blood starts oozing out, allow it to fall on the three circles of the glass slide by gently pressing the fingertip.
- Apply pressure on the site where it was pricked and to stop blood flow. Use the cotton ball if required.
- Mix the blood sample gently with the help of a toothpick and wait for a minute to observe the result.

Here is the chart which predicts the different types of blood groups along with its Rh factor (Table 10.1).

Table 10.1: Different types of Blood Groups

Blood Type	A	B	O	AB
Rh-positive	A+	B+	O+	AB+
Rh-negative	A-	B-	O-	AB-

As mentioned above, there are four major blood groups and eight different blood types, collectively called the ABO Blood Group System. The groups are based on the presence or absence of two specific antigens and antibodies– A and B.

1. Group A- Antigen A and Antibody B.
2. Group B- Antigen B and Antibody A.
3. Group AB- Antigen A and B both and no Antibodies
4. Group O- No Antigens and both A and B Antibodies.

Other than this, there is a third kind of antigen called the Rh factor. Based on the presence or absence of this antigen (Rh factor), the four blood group are classified into eight different blood types. If antigen D is present then blood group is Rh positive. and if Ag D is absent then blood group is Rh negative.

ESTIMATION OF HEMOGLOBIN BY SAHLI'S METHOD

Results: The given sample contains ——— blood group.

Practical 2nd: Estimation of hemoglobin.

Aim: To estimate hemoglobin by Sahil's method in a given sample.

Theory: Blood is mixed with N/10 HCl resulting in the conversion of Hb to acid hematin which is brown in cold. The solution is diluted till its color matches with the brown colored glass of the comparator box, the concentration of Hb is read directly.

Requirements: Haematometer which consists of comparator box having brown color on each side, Hb pipette marked up to 20 mm^3, tube with markings of Hb on one side glass rod, dropper, N/10 HCl, distilled water, blood sample.

Procedure:

1. Add N/10 HCl into the tube up to mark 2 g %.
2. Mix the EDTA sample by gentle inversion and fill the pipette with 0.02 ml blood. Wipe the external surface of the pipette to remove any excess blood.
3. Add the blood into the tube containing HCl. Wash at the contents of the pipette by drawing in and blowing out the acid two to three times and the blood is fixed with acid thoroughly.
4. Allow stand undisturbed for 10 min.
5. Place the haemoglobinometer tube in the comparator and add distilled water to the solution drop by drop stirring with the glass rod till its color matches with that of comparator glass. While, matching the color, the glass rod must be removed from the solution and held vertically in the tube.
6. Remove the stirrer and take the reading directly by noting the height of the diluted acid hematin and expresses in g%.

ESTIMATION OF HEMOGLOBIN BY CYANMETHEMOGLOBIN METHOD

Result: The hemoglobin of the given sample is ——— gm.

Practical 3rd: Hemoglobin estimation by cyanmethemoglobin method.

Aim: Estimation of hemoglobin by cyanmethemoglobin method

Requirements: Hb pipette, spectrophotometer, blood sample, Drabkin's solution pH 7.0-7.4 which contains potassium cyanide 50 mg, potassium ferricyanide 200 mg, potassium dihrogen phosphate 140 mg, nanionic detergent 1 ml, distilled water.

Theory: In this method, blood is diluted in a solution containing potassium cyanide and ferricyanide. The latter converts Hb to methemoglobin which is converted to cyanmethemoglobin (HiCN) by potassium cyanide. The absorbance of the solution is then measured in a spectrophotometer at a wavelength of 540 nm or in a colorimeter using a yellow green filter.

Procedure:

1. Take 5 ml of Drabkin's solution in a teat tube.
2. Mix the blood sample by gentle inversion and draw 0.02 ml of blood into the Hb pipette. Wipe the outer surface of the pipette to remove excess blood.
3. Place the pipette into the tube containing Drabkin's solution and slowly expel the blood into the solution. Mix well and let it stand undisturbed for 5 min.
4. Measure the absorbance of this solution at 540 nm in a spectrophotometer after adjusting the OD at by using Drabkin's solution as a blank.
5. Calculate the hemoglobin concentration using a standard curve.

Preparation of standard curve for hemoglobin estimation by cyanmethemoglobin method: In a laboratory which tests several samples in a day., it is more convenient to prepare a standard curve for Hb. WHO international reference Hi CN standard is available commercially as 10 ml sealed ampoules. This solution is stable for three years and the exact concentration of Hb present in the solution is indicated on the label (Fig. 10.1).

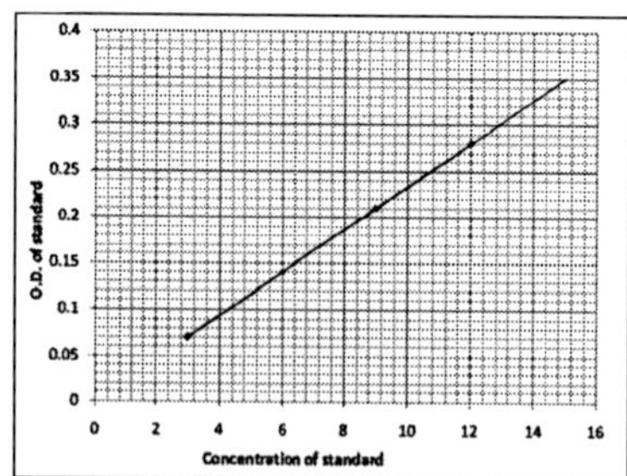

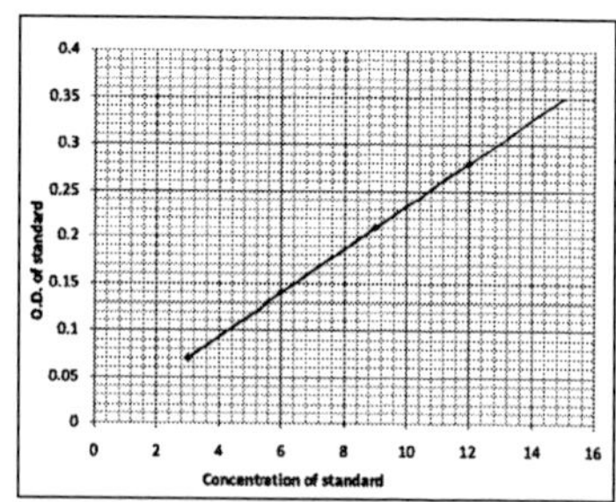

Fig. 10.1: Standard Curve

Preparation of standard curve:

1. Make a serial dilution of the reference solution eg. 1 in 2, in 1 in 4, 1 in 8 and so on with Drabkin's solution. As, the Hb present in the solution is known, the Hb concentration of each dilution will also be known.
2. Take the OD of each dilution in the colorimetry against a blank of Drabkin's solution.
3. Plot the OD against Hb concentration on a linear graph paper. The absorbance is plotted is plotted on the vertical axis.
4. From this graph, a table of reading and the corresponding Hb value can be prepared. This is more convenient than the graph as specially when a large number of readings have to be taken, the corresponding Hb value can be directly read from the table.

PROCEDURE FOR WHITE CELL COUNT

Practical 4th: WBC count

Aim: To perform total count of WBC

Theory: WBC is an enumeration of white corpuscles or is a leukocyte count. WBCs are composed of nucleoprotein and varieties of enzymes. Their number is less and life span is short as compared to red blood cells. The WBCs exist in two forms viz, granulocytes which are further classified as eosinophil, basophil, neutrophil and agranulocytes which are classified as lymphocytes and monocytes. The basic principle is that the blood is diluted with acid solution which removes the red cells by hemolysis and also accentuates the nuclei of white cells, thus the counting of the white cell becomes easy.

Requirements: Neubaur chamber, WBC pipette, cover slip, WBC diluting fluid. Needle, sprit and cotton.

Procedure:

1. Sterilize the fingertip with cotton plug soaked in 70 % alcohol and let it dry.
2. Take a bold prick to have free flow of blood and draw the blood in a WBC pipette up to 0,5 marks.
3. Dip the WBC pipette in WBC diluting fluid up to 11 make and rotate the pipette equally in your hands to mix the solution well by swirling.
4. Take the hemocytometer and place it on the flat surface of work bench.
5. Place the cover slip on the counting chamber and allow a small drop of dilute blood, hanging from the pipette, to sweep into the counting chamber by capillary action.
6. Make sure that there is no air bubble and there is no overfilling beyond the ruled area.
7. Leave the counting chamber on the bench for 3 minutes to allow the cells to settle. Observe the cells by placing the counting chamber on the mechanical stage of the microscope.
8. Focus on one of the corner squares of the counting chamber and count the white cells schematically, starting from the upper left small square of each square.
9. Repeat the count in all the four corners of the chamber (Fig. 10.2). Apply the margin rules i.e. count the cells lying on two adjacent margins and discard those on the other two margin.

Calculations: Volume of 1 square 1mm × 1 mm × 0.1 mm= 0.1 cmm

Volume of four squares = 0.4 cmm

If total number of leucocytes counted is Y (i.e. total cells counted in $L_1+L_2+L_3+L_4$) i.e. Y number of leukocytes counted in 0.4 cmm. So, in 1 cm there will be -y X 20 X 1/0.4

Leucocytes/cmm = Y X 50 cells/cmm

Leucocyte count = ... cells/cmm

Result: The number of WBC in own blood is .... per cubic mm.

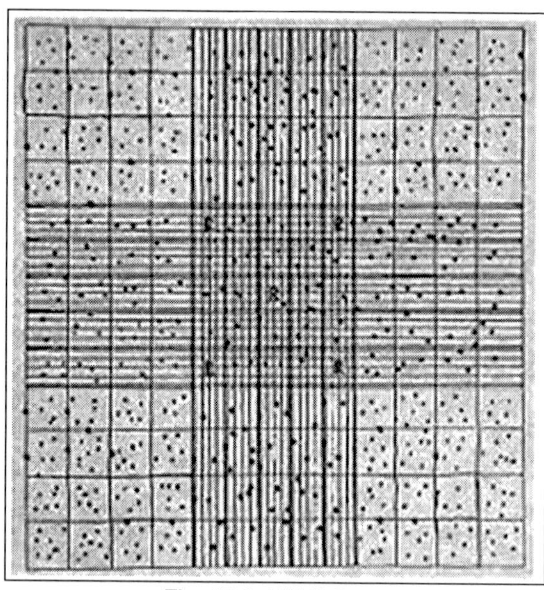

Fig. 10.2: WBC Counter

PROCEDURE FOR RED CELL COUNT

Practical 5th: RBC count

Aim: To perform total count of RBC

Hemocytometer: It consists of pipette and a counting chamber, pipette with large bulb having red bead in it and 101 mark is used for RBC count. The counting chamber most commonly used in Neubaur chamber. Neubaur's chamber is an H shaped bar on either side of which there are 9 squares (1mm X 1mm) each center square is also 1 sq mm. then center square is divided into 25 equal squares, the area of each square is 1/25 sq.mm. This small square is again divided into 16 small squares, hence area of each will be 1/400 sq.m.

Principle: The enumeration of blood cells is a fundamental method in the clinical laboratory. Normal red cells are biconcave disc which enclose hemoglobin. They have an average diameter of 7.3 µm, are non-nucleated and function to carry O_2 from lung to tissue and CO_2 from tissue to lung. Normal range of RBC is 4.5-6.0 million/ cubic mm in adult female. To, count total number of RBC, blood is diluted with a special thoma pipette and using isotonic diluting fluid. This diluted blood is placed in special counting chamber and cells in measured volume are counted or calculated.

Hayem's diluting fluid=0.5 gm mercuric chloride + 5gm $NaSO_4$ + 200 ml distilled water

Material requirements: H_2O_2, alcohol, ether, compound microscope, pricking needle, hayem's diluting fluid, RBC pipette hemocytometer (Neubaur's chamber).

Procedure:

1. Disinfect the finger tip with alcohol and wipe dry.
2. Puncture your middle finger of left hand so that blood may start oozing.
3. Draw the blood by sucking up to exactly 0.5 marks of thoma pipette.
4. Now, suck diluting fluid in such a way that volume in pipette may become up to 101 mark.
5. Shake well pipette to mix blood and diluting fluid perfectly
6. Put a drop of fluid in such a way that it may come on both scales situated on either side of horizontal of 'H'.
7. Put a coverslip on slide in such a way that it may cover both scales.
8. Leave the slide for 5 min and the count RBC in 5 small squares.
9. Calculate the average number of counts in all squares.

Basic Formula

Total cells per cmm = No. of cells counted X Dilution Factor/Area Counted X Depth Factor

EXAMINATION OF FLOCCULATION REACTION USING VDRL TEST

Practical 6th: VDRL test

Aim: To examine flocculation reaction using VDRL

Theory: The venereal disease research laboratory (VDRL) test is a non-treponemal micro flocculation test which is used for screening of syphilis. It detects the IgM and IgG antibodies to lipoidal material released from damaged host cells, as well as to lipoprotein like material and possibly cardiolipin released from the treponemes.

Material Required: VDRL slide, VDRL antigen, positive control serum, negative control serum, disposable droppers, disposable applicator applicator sticks.

Procedure: The procedure is carried out in the following manner-

1. Bring, the VDRL antigen suspension controls and samples to room temperature.
2. Pipette one drop (50µl) of the test specimen, positive and negative controls onto separate reaction circles of the disposable slide.
3. Add one drop of well-mixed VDRL antigen next to the test specimen, positive control and negative control.
4. Using a mixing stick mix the test specimen and VDRL antigen thoroughly spreading uniformly over the reaction circle.
5. Rotate the slide gently and continuously either manually or on a mechanical rotor at 180 rpm.
6. Observe for flocculation microscopically at 8 minutes.

Result Interpretation: The result can be interpreted as following-

(a) Reactive: If Ag-Ab clump of large or medium size then it is reported as reactive (positive VDRL test)

(b) Weakly Reactive: If antigen and antibody complex is small sized, it is weakly reactive.

(c) Non-Reactive: If no antigen antibody clump is formed, it is non-reactive.

WIDAL TEST

Practical 7th: WIDAL Test

Aim: To observe the agglutination reaction using WIDAL test.

Theory: Bacterial suspension which carry antigen will agglutinate an exposure to antibodies to *Salmonella* organisms. Patients suffering from enteric fever would possess antibodies in their sera which can react and agglutinate serial doubling dilutions of killed, colored *Salmonella* antigens in a agglutination test. The main principle of Widal is that if homologous antibody is present in patients serum, it will react with respective antigen in the reagent and gives visible clumping on the test card and agglutination in the tube.

The test will detect the presence or absence of following antigens-

1. 'H' Ag (flagellar Ag of Salmonella typhi)
2. 'O' Ag (Somatic Ag of Salmonella typhi)
3. 'AH' Ag (flagellar Ag of Salmonella para typhi A)
4. 'BH' Ag (flagellar Ag of Salmonella para typhi)

Requirements: Widal test kit, incubator, normal saline, refrigerator, application stick, graduated pipette.

Procedure: The procedure is carried out in following manner-

1. Place one drop of positive control on one reaction circle of the slide.
2. Pipette one drop isotonic saline on the next reaction circle (negative control).
3. Pipette one drop of the patient serum to be tested onto the remaining four reactions circles.

4. Add one drop of Widal test antigen (Ag) suspension 'H' to the first two reactions circles.
5. Add one drop each of 'O', 'H'. 'AH' and 'BH' antigens to the remaining four reaction circles.
6. Mix contents of each circle uniformly over the entire circle with separate mixing sticks.
7. Rock the slide, gentle back and forth and observe for agglutination within one minute.

Result Interpretation: The result is interpreted as-

1. Positive Test: Agglutination within a minute
2. Negative Test: No agglutination

Experiment 9: Enzyme linked immunosorbent assay

Theory: Enzyme Linked immunosorbent assay (ELISA) is a method is a method of capturing target antigen (Ag) or antibody (Ab) in samples using a specific Ab or Ag and detection or quantification using an enzyme reaction with substrate. In ELISA, various Ag-Ab combinations are used, always including an enzyme labeled Ag or Ab and enzyme activity can be measured using a substrate that changes color when modified by the enzyme. Light absorbtion of the product formed after substrate addition is measured and converted to numeric values. Depending on the Ag-Ab combination, the assay is called a direct ELISA, indirect ELISA, sandwich ELISA, competitive ELISA etc.

Direct ELISA: A large protein is immobilized on the surface of microplate wells and is incubated with an enzyme labeled antibody to the target protein. After washing the activity of the microplate well bound enzyme is measured.

Indirect ELISA: A target protein is immobilized on the surface of microplate wells and is incubated with an antibody to the target protein, followed by secondary Ab. After washing, the activity of the micro-plate, well bound and enzyme labeled antibodies are measure. Although indirect ELISA requires more steps than direct ELISA, labelled secondary Ab are commercially available eliminating the need to label primary Ab.

Sandwich ELISA: An antibody to a target is immobilized on the surface of microplate wells and incubated first with the target protein and then with another target protein-specific antibody, which is labeled with an enzyme. After washing, the activity of the microplate well-bound is measured and the immobilized antibody along with the enzyme labelled antibody which must recognize different epitopes of the target protein.

Competitive ELISA: An Ab specific for target protein is immobilized on the surface of microplate wells and incubated with samples containing the target protein and a known amount of enzyme labeled target protein. After the reaction, the activity of microplate well-bound enzyme is measured. When Ag level in the sample is high, the level of Ab bound enzyme labeled Ag is lower and the color is lighter. Conversely, when it is low the level of Ab bound enzyme labeled Ag is higher and the color is darker. After, the reaction the activity of the microplate well-bound enzyme is measured, when the antigen level in the sample is high, the level of Ab bound enzyme labeled Ag is lower and the color is lighter. Conversely, when it is low the level of Ab bound enzyme labeled Ag is higher and the color is darker.

Requirements: DOT ELISA Strip, 10 X assay buffer (phosphate buffered saline between-PBST) Ab-HRP conjugate, 10 X TMB/H_2O_2 buffer, test serum samples.

Procedure: The procedure is followed in the following manner-

1. Required amount of 10X assay buffer is diluted to 1 X with distilled water before use.
2. Test serum sample which should be reconstituted with 0.3 ml of distilled water.
3. In a viral take 1 ml of 1 X assay buffer and 50 ml of serum sample, mix throughout insert a DOT ELISA strip.
4. Allow the reaction to occur at room temperature for 20 minutes.

5. Wash the strip 3 times by dipping it in 1 ml of 1 X assay buffer for about 5 min each, replace the buffer each time.
6. Take 1 ml of 1 X assay buffer in a fresh vial, add 10 ml Ab HRP conjugate to it and mix throughout. Dip the strip and allow the reactions to take place fro 20 min.
7. Wash the strip as in (5) 3 times.
8. In fresh vial, take 0.1 ml of 10 X TMB/H_2O_2 and 0.9 ml of distilled H_2O and mix throughout, dip the strip in this substrate solution.
9. Observe the strip after 10-20 min for appearance of blue/grey spot.
10. Rinse the strip with distilled water

Observation: The observations are performed as follows-

(a) **Negative Control Zone:** In this zone, immobilized AB is not present hence, there is no reaction when reagents are added.

(b) **Positive Control Zone:** In this zone, Ag is bound to immobilize Ab and the Ag binds to Ab enzyme conjugate and spot is developed.

(c) **Test Zone:** In this zone, Ab is immobilized and colored spot is observed only when Ab specific Ag is present in the test sample (Fig. 10.3).

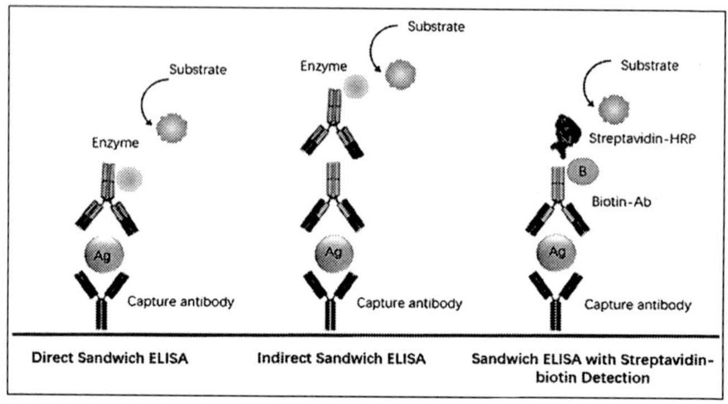

Fig. 10.3: Different types of ELISA

Glossary

1. **Antigen (Ag):** Antigen may be defined as a foreign particle, which is generally a protein and has the ability to combine with final product of immune response (i.e. Ab).
2. **Antibody (Ab):** Antibody may be defined as the final product of immune response which is a protein synthesized in response to Ag entered in the body, and is capable of fighting with the Ag and eliminating the Ag out of the body.
3. **Adjuvants:** It may also be defined as a substance which can increase the antigenicity or immunogenicity of the antigen, when adjuvant is added in vaccine it increases the antibody production of the body.
4. **Acquired Immunity:** An immune response generated by the body when any antigen enters in the body activating the immune system of the body to produce immune response in an individual.
5. **Agglutination:** It is an Ag-Ab reaction in which Ag and Ab aggregate to form Clumps.
6. **Allergen:** A substance that produces allergy is called allergen.
7. **Allergy:** It is referred as over immune response produced in 10% individuals which results in severe tissue damage, it is also known as hypersensitivity.
8. **Allograft:** Graft exchanged between two genetically dissimilar individuals of same species is known as allograft.

9. **Anaphylaxis:** Anaphylaxis or type I hypersensitivity is defined as an over immune response of the immune system where a sensitized animal encounters the Ag for the second time and this contact leads to degranulation of cells finally leading to the release of vasoactive substances that can damage different body tissues.
10. **Antibody Combining Site:** The structure present on an Ab molecule which links with a corresponding antigenic determinant or Epitope.
11. **Antigen-Antibody Complex:** Immune complex formed between Ag and Ab molecule when they bind together, there may be soluble or precipitating in nature.
12. **Antigenic Determinant/Epitope:** It refers to a particular site on Ag where the Ab binds to the Ag.
13. **Antigenicity:** The capacity of an Ag to combine with the Ab is called antigenicity.
14. **Autograft:** Transplant of a tissue from one site to other (within one's own body) is called autograft.
15. **Autoimmune Disease:** It refers to an autoimmune disorder which arises due to immunological destruction of tissues or their product on the host. It generally results by reaction between autoantigen and autoantibodies.
16. **Affinity:** The binding strength of a single epitope of the Ag to the single antigen binding site of the antibody is called affinity.
17. **Avidity:** The binding strength of all the epitopes of the antigen with all the antigen binding sites of the antibody is known as avidity.
18. **B cell:** It refers to Bone-marrow derived lymphocyte, which matures in Bursa of Fabricius in birds and in Bone-marrow in mammals.
19. **Cell Mediated Immunity:** An immune reaction mediated by T lymphocytes and their products, it is an independent reaction mediated by T cells only.

20. **Complements:** Complements are large, thermo labile, enzymatic proteins found in blood serum and body fluid activated by Ag-Ab complexes and they facilitate lysis, phagocytosis etc.
21. **Delayed Hypersensitivity:** It is an reaction mediated by T-lymphocytes and the visible manifestation of the reaction occurs in delayed hypersensitivity after 48 hours.
22. **Erythema:** Redness of the skin caused by inflammation reaction, redness is due to capillary enlargement or rupture.
23. **Fab region:** The Fab portion is that portion of Ab which contains paratope, it is located at the extremity of two limbs of Y, it contains a light and heavy chain fragment that can be separated by enzymatic digestion. It may also be defined as a portion which binds to the antigen.
24. **Fc fragments:** A fragments of Ab responsible for the binding of Ab and C1q complements to Ab receptors of cells and is generally that portion of antibody which does not bind to the Ag.
25. **Haemolysis:** Rupture or lysis of RBC is known as haemolysis.
26. **Heptane:** It is defined as small molecule which is antigenic and becomes immunogenic after binding with carrier proteins.
27. **Hashimoto's Disease:** It is a specific lesion in the thyroid involving infiltration of mononuclear cells.
28. **Helper Cells:** It refers to a class of T helper cells which contains CD4 marker and is the chief cell that works for the generation immune response.
29. **Histocompatibility Antigens:** They are genetically identified iso-antigens which are present on the membrane of nucleated cells but when introduced into another animal through graft transplantation, they are capable of producing an immune response leading to the rejection of the transplanted graft.

30. **Histocompatibility genes:** The genes controlling the formation of histocompatibility complex.
31. **Human Leukocyte Associated Complex (HLA):** It is a cluster of genes located on chromosome number 6 and they control the production of cell surface Ag called MHC Ag.
32. **Humoral Immunity:** The type of immunity generated by the joint coordination of T helper cells and B cells leading to the formation of Ab is known as humoral immunity.
33. **Hypersensitivity:** It is a type of over immune response generated by the immune system.
34. **Idiotype:** The antigenic characteristic of variable region of an Ab.
35. **Immune Response:** The response of body toward any pathogen entered in the body.
36. **Immunity:** The resistance of body against any particular disease.
37. **Immunization:** The production of protection against a pathogen either by the administration of Ag or by transfer of Ab.
38. **Immunocompetence:** The capacity of a host to produce a normal immune response to an Ag.
39. **Immunodeficiency:** A deficiency state involving one or more component of immune system.
40. **Immunoglobulin:** It is structurally similar to Ab and are Y shaped in structure, they are either secretary in nature or remain membrane bound on the cell.
41. **Immunofluorescence:** A technique for visualizing Ag-Ab reactions by conjugating one of them with a fluorochrome agent.
42. **Immunogen:** An Ag that is capable of eliciting an immune response in the body, i.e. it is capable of stimulating the body to produce Ab in is called immunogen.

43. **Immunological Tolerance:** The loss of capacity of the immune system to react with a particular Ag on subsequent encounters.
44. **Immunosupression:** Generalized suppression of the immune system caused by drugs, diseases, poor nutritious status, irradiation etc.
45. **Immunotheraphy:** Treatment of disease by immunization is called immunotherapy.
46. **Interferon:** It is a glycoprotein secreted by virus infected cell in order to induce anti-viral state in the neighbouring cells.
47. **Interleukins:** They are regulatory proteins secreted by monocytes, macrophages or activated TH cells which mainly function to communicate between the cells of immune system.
48. **Isotype:** They refer to different classes of immunoglobulins, having same antigenic specificity which are generated when same variable region of the immunoglobulin chain binds with different constant region of the heavy chain.
49. **Lymphocyte:** A lymphocyte refers to a class a WBC which are mostly agranulocytes with a diameter of 12mm or more and are derived by immune stimulation, they mainly consist of T cells, B cells and Null cells.
50. **Lymphokines:** They are soluble, non-specific substance other than Ab secreted by sensitized T cells to mediate cell mediated immunity, they are also secreted by B cells in the presence of T cells in culture.
51. **Kupffer Cells:** They are the macrophages found in liver which engulf Ag through the gut.
52. **Macrophages:** They are special type of antigen presenting cells, which are derived from monocytes and exhibit the property of phagocytosis and adhesion.
53. **Mast cell:** They are non-motile connective tissue cells on which the IgE antibody binds and when Ag enters

in the body for the second time the IgE linked mast cell degranulate leading to the release of histamines that are responsible for damaging the tissues of the body.

54. **Memory Cells:** Memory cells are a class of B cells which are responsible for storing memory for a particular disease. They also store pre-formed antibodies for specific pathogens, so that when the pathogen actually enters the pre-formed antibodies are ready to fight with the pathogen.
55. **MHC Genes:** The major histocompatibility complex (MHC) genes are the genes which code for MHC antigens such as HLA antigen of man or the H-2 antigen of mouse.
56. **Monoclonal Antibody:** Monoclonal antibodies or MAb refer to the antibodies produced against specific antigenic determinant.
57. **Monocyte:** A large, mononuclear, mobile, phagocytic white blood cell of bone-marrow origin.
58. **Natural Killer cells (NK):** Cells present in the lymphoid system that can kill target cells such as immune cells, bacteria, etc.
59. **Neutrophil Leucocyte:** A highly motile, short lived phagocytotic white blood cell of the myeloid series with cytoplasmic granules which does not take acidic or basic dye rather takes neutral stain.
60. **Non-specific immunity:** It is also known as innate immunity, it refers to the immunity present from birth and does not require recognition of a specific Ag.
61. **Null Cells:** They refer to a class of lymphocytes which originate in bone marrow and develop into NK and killer cells they are known to exhibit antiviral properties.
62. **Opsins:** They are the substances which bind to an antigen and makes its phagocytosis easier.
63. **Opsonisation:** The process of coating a cell with opsins like Ab or complements is known as opsonisation.

64. **Paratope:** The part of an Ab which binds with the antigenic determinants (epitope) of an Ag is known as a paratope.
65. **Passive Immunity:** Immunity that is transferred from an immune to a non-immune host so, that latter is temporarily immune to the Ag concerned.
66. **Pathogenicity:** The capacity of an organism or its products to cause disease is known as pathogenicity.
67. **Peripheral lymphoid Organs:** They are also known as secondary lymphoid organs and are those organs where the antigen come in contact with the lymphocytes.
68. **Phagocyte:** A cell which is able to ingest particulate matter.
69. **Phagocytosis:** It refers to the process by which macrophage eats other cells, it is also known as cell eating.
70. **Phagosome:** The digestive vacuole formed inside a phagocyte is known as phagosome.
71. **Plasma:** The fluid portion of un clotted blood is known as plasma.
72. **Plasma Cells:** It is a type of B cell which produces antibodies, they are found in spleen, lymphocyte and at the site of inflammation.
73. **Precipitation:** The formation of visible complexes in a solution or in clear semi-solid medium such as agar gel is known as precipitation.
74. **Precipitin:** An antibody which precipitates an antigen is known as precipitin.
75. **Primary Immune Response**: An primary immune response arises due to the first contact with the Ag. 76.
76. **Primed or Sensitized Animal:** An animal which has previously encountered and reacted to an Ag and therefore carries memory cells for response to such an Ag in future is known as primed or sensitized animal.

77. **Radioimmunoassay:** Radioimmunoassay or RIA refers to a method of measuring Ag or Ab using radiolabelled reagent.
78. **Reaginic Antibody:** It refers to the Ab which fixes to the mast cell releases vasoactive amines from mast cells or basophils, IgE is a type of reagnic Ab.
79. **Recognition Site:** The location of Ag receptor on a lymphocyte which allows the recognition of host.
80. **Self-Antigen:** Ag derived from one's own tissue is called self-antigen.
81. **Sensitization:** Exposure of a host to an Ag so as to induce an immune response with memory.
82. **Sensitized Cell:** A cell which has reacted with its specific Ab.
83. **Sensitized Lymphocyte:** A lymphocyte which has been antigenically primed is known as a sensitized lymphocyte.
84. **Serum:** The fluid portion from clotted blood, i.e. plasma minus fibrinogen, prothrombin, factor V. and VII, or clotting factor is known as serum.
85. **Serum Sickness:** It is the type III hypersensitivity reaction caused by formation of large immune complexes which get deposited on different body tissues leading to various types of reactions.
86. **T Cell:** It refers to thymus derived lymphocyte which is the main cell of immune system and is responsible for generation of cell mediated immunity.
87. **Transplant Ag:** The cell surface Ag which are responsible from graft rejection are known as transplant Ag.
88. **Transplantation:** The process of giving organ from one person to other is known as transplantation.
89. **Transplantation Rejection:** When organ of one person is given to other if their MHC do not match one person's organ is rejected in others body this is known as transplantation rejection.

90. **Vaccination:** It refers to the exposure of the host to certain live dead, or detoxified agent to induce active immunity to them or their pathogenic counterparts.
91. **Vaccine:** Vaccine may be defined as a dilute form of an antigen or immunogen, administered in the body in order to provoke antibody synthesis against the immunogen administered in the body.
92. **Vasoactive Amines:** Substances such as 5-hydroxytryptamine and histamines, which cause vasodilatation and increase vascular permeability are known as vasoactive substances.
93. **Xenograft:** It is also referred as heterograft tissue, used for grafting between organisms of different species

Index